WE WER ......⌐⌐ΓⱯⱾ

The Night Visitors (with Jenn Ashworth)

WE WERE STRANGERS

STORIES INSPIRED BY UNKNOWN PLEASURES

EDITED BY RICHARD V. HIRST

First published in 2018 by Cōnfingō Publishing

2 Stonecroft Court, Parkfield Road South, Didsbury, Manchester, M20 6DA
www.confingopublishing.uk

Art Direction & Typesetting by Zoë McLean
Printed by TJ International Ltd

A CIP catalogue record for this book is available from the British Library

ISBN 978-0-9955966-1-0

2 4 6 8 10 9 7 5 3 1

For Vincent, Maeby and Helen

In memory of Mark Fisher and Mark E. Smith

CONTENTS

We Were Strangers is an anthology of ten short stories by ten authors, each of which takes its title and inspiration from one of the tracks on Joy Division's debut album, *Unknown Pleasures*, and responds to its themes, texture and imagery.

Joy Division were a group from Manchester that consisted of Ian Curtis (vocals, lyrics), Peter Hook (bass), Stephen Morris (drums) and Bernard Sumner (guitars, keyboards). They formed in 1976 and went on to record two studio albums. Curtis suffered from depression and epilepsy and committed suicide in May 1980, aged 23. The remaining members re-formed under the name New Order, achieving global success and acclaim.

Unknown Pleasures was recorded in April 1979 and released in the summer of that year. It's difficult to say precisely what it is that makes the record so important to so many people. The songs which make up *Unknown Pleasures* are dark – brooding and ominous both in lyric and composition – but pop has always been a home for darkness: Leonard Cohen's *Songs of Love and Hate* springs to mind, as do Nico's *The Marble Index* and the recordings from David Bowie and Iggy Pop's Berlin period. What sets *Unknown Pleasures* apart is its singular, beguiling vision. Like a lot of great art, it is concerned with the tensions of sustained contradictions. Here is a record of grand, mythic darkness made by four men in their early 20s with the same life experiences, finances and instruments at their disposal as any other group; it is bleak – obsessively morose and despondent – yet also affirming and thrilling; it is catchy pop yet characterised by a rare and unmannered seriousness: funeral music that you can dance to.

Why short stories? Writers have been drawn to Joy Division since *Unknown Pleasures* was first released. 'It's so incredibly dark,' Irvine Welsh once said of the record, 'yet awesome and powerful.' 'To me,' wrote Ian Rankin, 'there's almost a narrative running through *Unknown Pleasures*.' Indeed, Ian Curtis's legacy lies principally in his distinctive lyrics, suggestive as they are of some kind of story, a chronicle of isolation, anguish, biblical conflict and ecstasy, but one whose plot, characters and structure are all lost in the dark and the fog. The listener feels a temptation to shade in between the lines of Curtis's oblique words and the group's cavernous melodies, a flame lit in their imagination. What better medium than the short story – a form currently enjoying an uncanny renaissance – to discover what that blaze will illuminate? The short story is the obscure side-street arena for our fascination with the inexplicable and the aberrant, necessitating as it does ellipses, the power of apparent non sequiturs and, always, mystery.

Manchester's most enduring post-war cultural contribution has been its pop music. That began, it could be argued, with Joy Division, and Joy Division began with *Unknown Pleasures*. Next year, 2019, the album will be 40 years old and with the passing of each of those 40 years, Joy Division have grown to seem not so much a pop group, and *Unknown Pleasures* not so much a record, as the means by which some dark energy first took hold of the listening consciousness. The following stories constitute a contemporary literary snapshot of the impact that energy has had: what we heard, what it has done for our imaginations, and where it has led us.

RICHARD V. HIRST, MANCHESTER, APRIL 2018

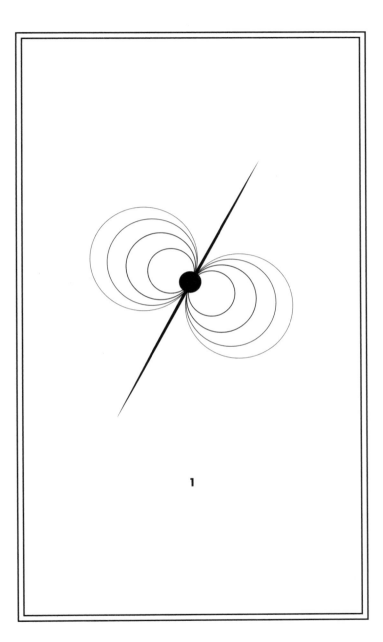

1

DISORDER

NICHOLAS ROYLE

The pain is back. Mine. More a sensation. You know, you remember. Control the feeling, beware the fear. Change what you can control. Control what you can't change. In the end, all is lost.

Start again.

Where will you find a different way, the right road? It takes time. Make time your friend. Oh yeah, all that. I've run from friends and talked to strangers, and walked out of the city, far into the night. I tried moving, but only in my heart. I travelled far, but obtained nothing. She had everything. You had everything. Attracted to myths, you surrendered to angels. Searching for God's glow, you sank to the depths.

Start again.

I campaigned hard. I just didn't know what for. To get a feeling, to see your hand. Get lost, you said. But where? On my own or with you? I broke you, you said, clinging, directionless. Me, not you. Control. I had to keep control. For me, you filled a room. You were my world. I lost friends. I lost the centre. I lost my edge. The hopes I had tried to hold on to lay around me, kicking as they died. You showed me the world in a room. A cage, a lost childhood, the end of everything, the values of nothing.

Again.

Of the streets, of the houses, of the windows, of the door. Of the shadowplay on the wall. The feeling in my dreams, the spirit of my youth. The times. The times I've travelled and lost. The times I've screamed in the night. The time I've lost, waiting for something, waiting for someone, waiting for you. We were just bodies, you said, of blood and skins. Where was the spirit?

Christ, the tears I cried. The strangers I found and gave to you as toys. Their cold, wide eyes and thin faces. Their silence. To you it was bloodsport. Some died, many were lost and many more will not remember. They cried as they lay there. You turned to me. Oh, their tears. What did you want? The tears. The blood and the tears. We looked for too long. The sense broke down. They were just bodies, and so we took them to places of darkness and despair. Was this the end? Were we lost?

The change was hard and violent. You demanded a gun. She's gone, I thought. Lost. Occupied by death. Corrupted by sin. Where could we go? What could we do? Where was the way out?

We were living in a little room with wide cracks in one wall. The building's windows were dark all the time, the nights long, each day the same. A lost voice cried, in the distance, No, no, no. No more. Marked strangers walked in the roads, with eyes down. The city felt far away. All through those lost nights children screeched, regrets were distorted, and feeling lost out to noise and fire and pain. Friends-turned-judges took control and gave little away any more. Eyes flashing, cars crashing.

I've seized on mistakes and tried to get free. I've turned people into martyrs and pleasures into sadness. I've lost the means to connect, the will to know the truth. I've seen crowds die. I remember watching a man's violent end and not feeling it. Looking at a knife and not seeing power.

Much longer ago, in forgotten youth, I tried to control strangers and so made friends. These were fatal errors for me. I travelled by train through unknown territories without a guide and got lost. I looked in the eyes of assassins and something died. Where could I get control? Where could I find knowledge? It's a prophet you are looking for, a voice said. Where will I find one? Where, where, where? It's not where but when. So when? When you are close to the end. How will I know? All the disbelief and confusion will fall away. You will see long and wide. You will understand.

The body is weak. There's violent pain and a metallic taste. No control. Then no sensation, apart from all the rust and the thin odour of steel. There's no escape, no way out.

The bodies, in a row, move only when they are disturbed.

In the distance, through deep time, for me, childhood ends. For there's no more time and I'm no longer young. Not any more. Where is there now? What is there now? I'm afraid I've lost the stomach for it. I'm too weak, too far gone.

All right?

No, not really, I said.

I've been looking on, outside, watching through the window. I saw one passer-by, and a second. I saw four, ten, twelve. Is there no end to this? Where are they going on to, these strangers? Where and when will these trials end? No, let me guess.

In the car, getting out of the city. On a neon trail, lost time, enormous prisons for young sons long trapped, goaded by strangers. Violent eyes, wasted feeling, never worked, angry tears. Meet your end. I don't feel any more, just look and remember. You wanted to know, what did I see? A last chance, for them. Torn bodies grouped on the floor, again, in the corner.

Again.

Time to get out. We loaded the car and travelled slowly, then faster, laughed as we were pulled over for our speed. Blue lights. Please step outside. For their eyes, for their fingers, for their bodies. For their control. For bloodsport. What a waste. To see the colours, to hear the sound, to feel the heat. To forget the moves and admire the spirit. To nail the feeling, to hold the sensation. To control the edge, to control the centre. To guess the end.

More bodies, for more control.

Will she lose interest? Can she keep secrets? The pressure is creeping up. I'm hoping, for me, it will all come to an end. The end of acting up, of looking lost, of moving on, of making do. What brought me here? What lies obtained my withdrawal from normal limits? Who were we in a different time? And from a different place? Where were we when, afraid, we tried to end it all? It's for her. It's for you. It's for her. It's for me. For mine. I've… I've seen friends share blame and strangers collect pity. I've set close friends (with habits, no saints) on the wrong way just to get some control. Different rules for strangers. A state of upheaval and a darker side. Forced tears, gaps in time, shown no clue. She's got her way. Again she's obtained control. She's trying a different line, she said. Soon we will know more. She will watch me and I will watch her. We'll each stare. It will all end and we will lose, again.

Pass me the phone… Hey. I— Yeah, sure. Yeah… Beside mine… No, too weak, too afraid… I get to meet too many… Where? Who by then? I've had mine for all of, well, since always… She may let me… Where were their—? Where now? … Right. Keep that. I know. That spirit… Damn it.

His friend, the fence... Where? ... When? Just a moment... Right. The tenth... Too wide and too frequent... Oh, where again? I think we're behind, though... Like, four sided, somehow... Special room for—? Use your senses to— Good. I had some in mine... There? Bed, sheets, floor. She had this place.

I'm told I guessed the right moment and you walked through the room. All that spirit and power and control. Until you lose it again, when you don't move any more, afraid of your own reaction, of looking lost.

She's distorted by drink, a waste. I saw it and walked away. The strain's getting too much. The end, within, the same but different. We'll take a chance. We've come this far and made some mistakes but obtained proof. Their ways are not a right any more. Beware a change, and a force, and a nature, and destroyed youth, and waste, and closed eyes and dancing, a waiting, a looking round, a knowing, a hoping, and wider, faster cars, the ocean getting warmer, dust, glory, inserted memory, style that's expressed with feeling, trying to take control, trying to lose control.

It gives way like low water. It takes control. It reflects on the past. It says, rise up. It slumps down. It means well.

I'm in shock. I saw it take some of me. I'm down there until I'm up here again. I've been afraid. I'll get better. I'll live.

You stare through me. I've had it with you. I made a move. Oh, I say, I did it again and I did it again and I did it again. I say, I don't know where this will end. Why can't I see it through to the end? She's guessed the right way. She's waiting again. She's obtained her own man. She's travelled on through time. She's filled with will. She's got to stop herself, got to close it, lose it. She's afraid she'd barely hold on.

You left around what time? To the nearest hour... But who with? Any more? ... Where else? ... The long way round... To who then? To another group? ... To where? On this side? ... On that side... Shined lights at? ... Yeah. Take your time... You saw your friend getting all cross? All right. Don't— Good. We don't care.

Keep control of new sensations. Act on urge in city centre. See portrait in plain style. Take stairs for pleasure. Descend by wire with own hand. Give control of motion to friend. Lose all feeling in hand. Think through new case. Treat fine lines in corner.

There were some leads long ago.

Shades of feeling seem to show more spirit.

Stay with the scene. Long takes. The spirit of the place. The feeling of the land. Wide view.

You saw all the red mess and edged through the room. I heard the chair upon the floor. You played your hand and I mine. We knew we had lost. Now I see the waste of it all. So many lost and some, who won't tell, still waiting. She'd had it all. In her way, did she care? Did she change?

I've talked for too long. But I've said it all. I have to live. Until there are no new sensations any more. Until the end.

How I wrote 'Disorder'

'Disorder' is made out of the lyrics to *Unknown Pleasures*, those words and no others. No quotation is used and no word is repeated unless it is repeated in the lyrics.

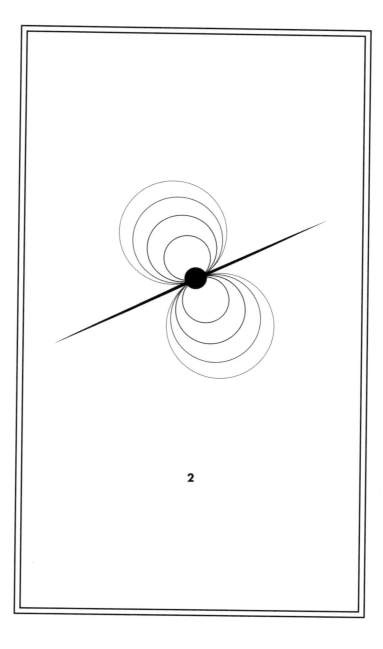

2

DAY OF THE LORDS

JENN ASHWORTH

The place was worse than the last time he'd seen it. The windows dirtier, the air inside imperceptibly heavier. Perhaps the roof had leaked over the winter. He scuffed through the mail in the communal hall, awkwardly holding the boy's hand. They climbed the stairs together, avoiding the worn red carpet along the centre of the tread. Rick's bedsit was on the third floor: not quite the top, but near enough. The whole building smelled like cellars.

Last time, he'd waited downstairs while Kath went up with the boy – her son – to do the drop-off. Now Kath was at work so he was here to do it himself. He used his free hand on the banister to haul himself upwards. It was uncomfortable, to be holding the boy's hand like this – and perhaps not quite right. It's what Kath would do, he reckoned. She was very safety-conscious. He squeezed the little hand again, sticky and hot, Ted clinging on to his fingers as they climbed the final flight of stairs. He didn't know what would be required of him when they reached the top.

He found the right door, which had the number daubed on in white paint and was fitted with a screwed-on plastic sign about the arrangements in the event of a fire – more like a hotel than a home, he thought – and paused. What state would the boy's father be in? The boy waited. He was zipped up tight in his red raincoat, the laces of his shoes done up in big bows: Kath's handiwork.

'You all set? You're going to have a nice day today. See your dad. He'll have been waiting for you.'

The boy said nothing, but kicked at the corner of the doormat with the toe of his shoe. Paul couldn't work him out. He must know the routine by now: dropped off on a Saturday morning, picked up in the evening. Like clockwork every week, no matter what. But here he was, dithering. Perhaps he didn't want to go in.

The father was a bit of a deadbeat. And *deadbeat*, in his opinion, was putting it mildly. No sign of him improving his circumstances so the boy could stay overnight. Paul had pushed for that, at first. For being able to take Kath away for a night or two. A whole weekend, even. It was only fair that the boy's father took his share of the responsibility. There was no money coming from him either. But Kath had resisted. 'It's better as it is,' she'd said, and he'd let it go. Not his place, of course. What did he know?

'OK, let's go,' Paul said, and banged on the door, and the thump he made echoed up and down the stairs and sounded harder and more aggressive than he meant it to. When Rick opened it, shirtless and barefoot, the top button of his jeans undone, the boy leapt forward and Paul was forced to release his hand. Rick's hair was a state and Paul glanced at his watch to cover up a frown.

'We're not early, are we?'

Rick rubbed his chin: days-old stubble there.

'No, no. It's me. Couldn't sleep last night.' He shrugged, smiled at Ted and tousled his hair. 'Come on then, get inside.'

The boy was not reluctant, and trotted past his father into the bedsit.

Paul handed the bag over.

'Change of clothes. Kath's put in a packed lunch. His drink, too. The Spider-Man bottle he likes.'

Rick squinted at the bag, then at Paul – as if he didn't recognise him.

'Kath told me to bring it. Just in case, you know, if you didn't have anything in for him.'

They had met before, once, a year ago. He and Kath were out at a pub – the boy on a rare sleepover with his grandmother. Rick had come in, steaming drunk, and it had spoiled their night.

It was that evening, in greenish glare from the numbers on the travel alarm clock Kath brought when she came to stay at his, she told him about Rick. About his anger. The punching of doors and walls.

'He only ever hurt himself,' she said. 'He never hit me. Never hit Ted. But I felt like it was only a matter of time, you know? And he wouldn't get himself sorted out. Drinking. Worse when he's had a skinful, of course, but not that great without it. So I went. It's made him worse, I think. Not having anyone to put the brakes on for.'

He had pressed her on this, and threatened to go around to wherever Rick – the *tosser* (that's how he thought of him, when he came to mind – never used his name, just *tosser*) – was and give him a talking-to. Show him who was in charge now. Show him that displays like the one at the pub that night – Rick weaving across the room to lean on their table, trying to start a fight over something to do with a box of vinyls he'd left behind and was now accusing Kath of selling or otherwise disposing of – would no longer be tolerated. That she was with him now, and any complaints she had, he'd be taking a personal interest in.

She'd poked him in his chest and laughed.

'Don't you get on your high horse about it, matey,' she'd said, still laughing, even though her eyes looked sad. 'He's just one of those people who've got to find an excuse to be angry. When we lived together, it was the noise the baby made, or the washing piling up, or tea not being ready on time. When I left, it was his old commanding officer, or the medical corps, or the journalists. Or his mother. Or the fact that I'd left. And now he can't go back out there, and his mother won't speak to him and his washing is his own problem. It's just his bloody vinyls. Keep well away – don't let him make you into his next excuse.'

Out there – he knew what that meant. The news had become more and more vague about the cause and location of the conflict, but he'd seen the illegal mobile-phone footage of the bombed-out buildings and burning cars on the internet, the same as everyone else had. The films sometimes showed queues at the medical tents, the bodies wrapped in sheets on the side of the road, helicopters in the United Army colours circling overhead. It was impossible to know which side to be on. You were supposed to show gratitude for their sacrifice no matter what your opinions on the conflict.

The soldiers who had come back, like Rick, were heroes and outcasts at the same time. They passed a couple of them on the way back from the pub that night: one sleeping in a doorway and another begging in his uniform in the town centre. He'd given the man money, just because Kath was watching and he'd wanted to make a good impression. But later, in bed, he'd been uncomfortably aware that he hadn't ever been *out there* himself, and not wanting the conversation to turn in that direction (he'd failed the fitness tests, then been exempted from the call-up for a technical reason he didn't understand), he'd let it go.

'He's Ted's father,' she'd said, 'whatever else he is. I don't want him growing up not knowing where he came from.'

'You know best,' Paul said. But he had not forgotten it.

He tried to look past Rick into the bedsit: to see what the boy was finding to do in there.

'No Kath today?' Rick said. So, they were going to make polite conversation, were they?

'That's right.'

There was a shuffling sound, a scraping – as if Ted was opening drawers or kitchen cupboards. He had a tendency towards that, at home – poking about in the kitchen and pulling the pans on to the floor. Kath allowed it. Said it did no harm and was his way of learning. Said the mess and the noise didn't matter. But inside the bedsit would there be medicine bottles unstoppered? Knives and broken glass lying about?

'Where is she?'

'She had to cover a shift. Called in first thing this morning. She did send a text to say it would be me.'

Rick was looking over his shoulder at the disturbance going on behind him. 'Ted? Not in there.'

Paul was reluctant to leave. Is this what it is, to be a parent? To feel as he did now – off-duty and released of his responsibility but unable to quite relax? Like a taxi parked at the kerb with the meter still running? Just like that.

'Well, I'll get off. It'll be me tonight too. About six all right?'

Rick nodded, still distracted.

'And you've got my mobile number? If anything…'

There was a crash from inside: the sound of breaking

glass. Paul pushed past Rick and into the bedsit, his body flying quicker than thought. He'd never been in here before and the room was only a blur to him as he flew through it in three strides. Dark. Poky. Cluttered and sparsely furnished. None of that mattered but Ted, who was sitting in a puddle and the smell of alcohol was thick and sharp in the dim room.

'Don't move. Keep still!' Paul shouted, leaned over, and plucked Ted up from the floor, the puddle, and the remains of a big bottle of black market vodka. Broken glass lay on the tiled floor around him.

'Are you cut? Let me see your hands,' Paul said, and brushed at the front of the boy's clothes. 'Come on. Your hands, Ted.'

He was speaking sharply – the anger he felt at the *tosser* creeping into his voice – and Ted turned his head away from him, cried, and would not speak. Rick crossed the room, treading gingerly through the wet in his bare feet, and Ted held out his arms to him. Paul let him go.

'Check him. Is he cut?'

It was too dark in the room to see much – Paul felt how wet the boy was and though he knew it was probably just the vodka, until he could be 100 per cent certain that there wasn't an artery or a major vein cut, he had to assume that the wetness was blood.

'Is he bleeding?'

He reached up to draw the curtain, which wasn't a curtain at all, only a bed sheet tied to the pole and tacked along the edge of the window frame with drawing pins. They popped out, one after the other, and skittered across the tiles. The light flooded in. There was no blood. Paul let all the air out of his lungs and, without meaning to, spoke.

'For fuck's sake,' he said, 'is this how you live?'

Rick had Ted in his arms, the boy's head tucked in under his chin. They fitted together like that easily and the boy was not hurt, and Ted was cowering away from Paul. Rick was patting his back, soothing him.

'He's not cut?'

'He's in one piece. Aren't you, son? In one piece. Course you are.'

'Right. Sorry. I panicked. Felt the wet and...' He looked again at the floor. The place stank. The bed – bare mattress and a duvet without a cover – took up most of the room. There was a laptop open on the draining board of the tiny kitchenette, books and magazines scattered across the floor. And a row of cups that had been used as ashtrays on the windowsill. On the walls, a couple of girly posters and some photographs of his army mates.

'Do you have a mop?'

'There's a bathroom in the hallway. I think I saw one in there once. Maybe a dustpan too.'

Ted had stopped crying, but remained tight in against his father's chest. Rick crossed the room and sat on the edge of the bed.

'I'll change his clothes in here. If you don't mind? Sorry. Bare feet.'

The shared bathroom was filthy, the toilet seat cracked and propped crookedly against the cistern. There was a poster above the toilet advertising the free walk-in clinic for returned United Army veterans in need of housing or financial advice. The mop – its head solidified with filth and old soap, looking like a brain – was missing its bucket, so Paul grabbed an old, grey-looking bath towel from a hook on the back of the door, returned to Rick's room, and used that to soak up the vodka. He collected the glass in a dirty soup bowl and left it on the draining board.

He seethed as he worked. *Tosser. Tosser. Tosser.* He was at once furious with Kath – for shackling herself to this man for the next fifteen years at least – and with Rick himself, for the bottle, and the glass, and the sheet against the window, and everything else. This was ex-forces housing – notoriously squalid and nothing like the plush pictures of hotel-style rooms shown in all the posters – but the man had options. All it took was some effort. Paul didn't have a son of his own and he still managed to make more of an effort than *this*. He threw a final piece of glass into the bowl. Rick had changed Ted's clothes and put the wet ones back in the bag. The pair were clinging to each other on the edge of the bed, Ted's knees drawn up close like a primate. He only shouted, he didn't hit him, for fuck's sake.

'Thanks for that, mate. No harm done, eh?'

Paul made a noise in his throat: neither agreement nor disagreement.

'Bin's under the sink.'

Rick was going to ask him to replace the bottle next, Paul thought, and ignored him. He could chuck the glass out himself.

'Shall I take his old clothes back with me? Get them washed?'

'That'd be good, thanks.'

The bag changed hands again. That done, there was nothing more to keep Paul, but still he lingered, furious and mistrustful.

'Here. Let me say goodbye to Ted. I don't like the thought of going while he's still upset with me.'

'He's not upset with you,' Rick said, but in a sing-song voice that immediately charmed a smile out of the boy. 'He's not upset with you, is he? No, he's not. He just had a bit of a scare. That's all. All that noise. But it's all tidied up now. All sorted out.'

Ted uncurled, mollified, and crawled down from the bed and on to the floor.

'Out? We're going out, Daddy?'

'As soon as I've got my kit on,' he replied.

And Paul still loitered there, redundant entirely.

'How did you do that?' he asked.

Rick had his back to him, taking a T-shirt from a hanger that was hooked on to the picture rail. He watched the tattoos on Rick's back – a snake wrapped around a sword, and the names and dates of some United Army mates that never came back – flex and ripple as he raised his arms and slipped the T-shirt over his head. He turned.

'You get the knack for it. Distracting them out of a tantrum. He once threw a fit in the supermarket and I told him there was a pigeon sitting up on one of the shelves, and he was scaring it. It kept him entertained for an hour, that one did.'

He forced his feet into his trainers.

'Well, Ted, come here and give me a hug.'

Ted obeyed, stiffly, but Paul knew there was no feeling in it. It hadn't been his department. Better, he'd always thought, to leave the boy to his mother. Better for the boy. Better for her. And for him too, he admitted. It wasn't his plan to be a father. He had no special feeling for children. No urge to leave his mark on the world in that way. But even though the crisis had passed, he imagined cut arteries and the boy's blood pooling on the floor and was appalled at the nearness of danger.

'It wasn't always like this,' Rick said, as if reading his mind. He gestured towards the photographs on the wall, sun-faded now, and still in their brown, gold-embossed cardboard frames from the photographer. 'I was different. I was all right. Before I went out there.'

Paul knew nothing about the United Army. About what the work was like, *out there*. Nothing that he hadn't learned from the *News at Ten* and the mobile-phone videos, which most people said were staged anyway. He knew what Kath had told him – that Rick got caught by the second call-up, and went away reluctantly to do something that he eventually came to believe in. He had a sense of responsibility, she said. He'd bought into all the leaflets and posters that urged the able-bodied to 'answer the call to protect the values and way of life' of those at home. Then he came back, and when he did he was so angry he'd started breaking chairs and punching holes in the walls.

'Was it the powder?' The United Army issued drugs, he knew, or thought he knew – to keep the soldiers steady while they answered the *call to protect*. There were side-effects.

'He doesn't remember if he got dosed. He just says he can't sleep now,' Kath said. 'He has bad dreams,' she frowned, as if trying hard to remember. 'It's like he brought something else back with him. A guest in his head.' She looked at him in such a way that Paul wondered if she'd had a visit from Rick's extra guest herself. The one he'd brought back in his kitbag from out there, and moved into their house. She'd stuck it out three years – through her pregnancy with Ted up until he was two and she felt it wasn't safe any more. And she would not be drawn further.

'Pass me his coat,' Rick said. Paul did, and stood uselessly as Rick set Ted down on his feet and gently fastened him into his raincoat. He picked up his wallet and keys from a chair by the bed. He was leaving, so Paul had to, too, and he followed them down the stairs, walking slowly – at Ted's pace – and listening as the boy counted each step. He didn't know he could make it past ten.

'You're a clever boy,' he said, impressed.

'Kath tells me that's you. You're the one with the head for sums.'

They were at the front door now. Outside, the sky was covered in cloud and there was a cool wind. Spring, yes, but the hair was up on Rick's arms and Paul wondered why he hadn't brought a coat. Probably hadn't got one. Left it in a pub or a park somewhere, probably. *Tosser.*

'I bought him a poster for his bedroom wall,' Paul explained. 'Sheep on it. Sheep jumping over fences. He's to count it when he's up in the night, to help him to get back to sleep.'

'Right,' Rick said. He was locking the door. The car was at the kerb and Paul had the urge to offer them a lift. The park, with the fountain and the café and the crazy golf and the aviary – where he knew they spent most of their Saturdays – was only ten minutes' walk away, but the car was right there, and it wasn't the best weather. 'He's up in the night?'

'Sometimes. Yes. He needs the toilet. He's crying for his mum. A glass of water. That sort of thing. Kids' stuff.'

'He's not having bad dreams?'

'He doesn't say he is,' Paul said. How strange it was to be giving an outline of Ted's inscrutable night-time hours to the boy's own father. He went through the nightly routine in his head: the egg-timer in the shape of a duck to time the tooth-brushing. A beaker with water in it, not milk, because milk could still rot your teeth, according to Kath – which was a new one on him. He'd had to learn how to do these things. To know which of the stuffed rabbits Ted liked to have in bed with him, and which lived on the shelf over the door, to guard against monsters. Did Rick know about all that?

'I wondered. What with you saying he was up in the night. They can be terrible. Bad dreams. Make you feel like you're in another world, or that this one has just ended. He's seen some stuff. Me and his mother. I know I wasn't always...' This was the longest speech that Paul had heard Rick make. 'I know there's room for improvement. Kath says you're a good help. That you're trying hard with him.'

'He's not said anything about the dreams. Doesn't mention you.'

Rick looked wounded at this, and, with the man's temper in mind, Paul attempted to correct himself. 'I mean, they aren't about you. The dreams. Probably just monsters. Dragons, or whatever.'

Paul made a note to himself: ask Kath not to talk about him to Rick. Not to say things like 'he's a good help' or 'he's trying hard' – as if he was the pupil, and she was the teacher, giving Rick a report on his performance. What would that make Rick then? His father? He frowned again. Rick was talking to him and he'd lost the thread of the conversation.

'I don't really remember what I dream about,' Rick was saying. 'Perhaps he gets that from me. I wake up – covered in sweat – fighting with the sheets. I near enough ripped my pillow in half one night.'

'How do you know you're dreaming, if you don't remember it?'

Kath was like that, Paul thought. Restless in her sleep. Sometimes patting at the blankets in the dark, as if trying to soothe or calm them.

'I get bits of it,' Rick said. 'Flashes. Fire. Feet stamping. A car. Blown up. Sometimes a baby crying,' he shook his head. 'They said I might get them. Once I came back. But I didn't know...' He let his voice tail away. 'I'm keeping you. Sorry.'

'The booze won't help. All that vodka. In the boy's reach too,' Paul said. 'I don't know what Kath is going to say...'

Rick sighed. 'She'll say what she always says – that I should get it together.'

Paul nodded, and as they were out in the street, with witnesses and passers-by – the soft hum of the county council drone passing overhead – he felt emboldened.

'She's right. You want to sort yourself out,' Paul said, but quietly, and in a nice tone – in case Ted was listening. 'For the boy's sake.'

'It wasn't the plan to end up like this. We were married. Me and Kath.'

Paul bristled at this, and Rick raised his hands, palms upturned.

'I know we can't go back. I'm not trying to. I know she's with you now. That's what I'm saying. That's fine. It's my problem to deal with. But I am telling you that this, how it is now – it wasn't my plan. Nobody says they want to be like this when they grow up.'

'Kath works like a dog. The hours she does at that care home. You wouldn't believe it. She's knackered all the time.' He waved a hand, to indicate not just the state of the bedsit, but of Rick's entire situation. 'You must think something of her. You clearly feel a lot for Ted.' Rick looked away and laughed quietly to himself at the stiff Englishman's euphemism for love, and Paul was embarrassed but carried on. 'So I don't understand why you wouldn't sort yourself out. For his sake.'

Paul clicked the central locking button on his key and got into his car. The radio crackled into life: the news. Another list of losses and casualties, phrased so as to imply progress in the conflict. The numbers were astonishing if you let yourself think about it too much. People said there'd be another call-up before the end of the year. Paul turned the radio off. Rick made a winding gesture with his hand and he lowered the window.

'I'm doing my best,' he said. There was a tone to his voice that Paul did not recognise. Tired. More than that. Beaten. 'He's my boy.'

'And I'm trying hard with him,' Paul said, mimicking Kath's words. Rick smiled.

'So I hear.'

They went. Ted didn't wave but Rick did, one hand raised as he turned away and walked with his son down the street. Paul watched them in the rear-view mirror until they turned and passed out of sight. The carrier bag of wet clothes rested in his lap.

'Was it all right?' Kath asked. 'Was Rick all right?'

The two of them hovered by the door, the sheep on the poster just visible in the dim night-light of the boy's room.

'Rick was fine. Best behaviour,' Paul whispered.

'I was worried.'

'No need. All in hand.'

Ted slept, his hair curled softly over his forehead. Paul thought it made him look like a girl, but Kath wouldn't have it cut.

'Not yet,' she said, when he offered to take Ted to his own barber's and get it sorted, 'let him be a baby for longer.'

Now Paul saw that if he did get it cut – cut really short, an army haircut like his dad's – well, he'd look just like him. Paul could see this; could see the shape of Rick's shoulders and jaw in miniature, laid on to the boy like a mould. He was going to be a big lad.

'He didn't cry?'

'It was fine. He went off fine,' Paul said. He'd already decided not to tell her. To make up some excuse about the clothes if she noticed them. He'd washed them in the kitchen sink and the smell of the vodka had come out more easily than he'd expected.

'I'm going to sit down. I'm done in,' she said. The living room door opened and closed. He heard the television through the thin wall. Something about a third call-up: either speculation about an announcement, or even the announcement itself. He did not strain to listen: there was no point in knowing. His letter would come at some point, he supposed. Kath changed the channel and called to him. 'You coming through, love?'

Paul lingered in the doorway for a minute longer, looking at the rapid rise and fall of the boy's chest under the Spider-Man duvet cover. He did not touch him, but just stayed like that, observing the way the boy's eyes moved under his eyelids, as if watching someone run back and forth across his field of vision as he slept.

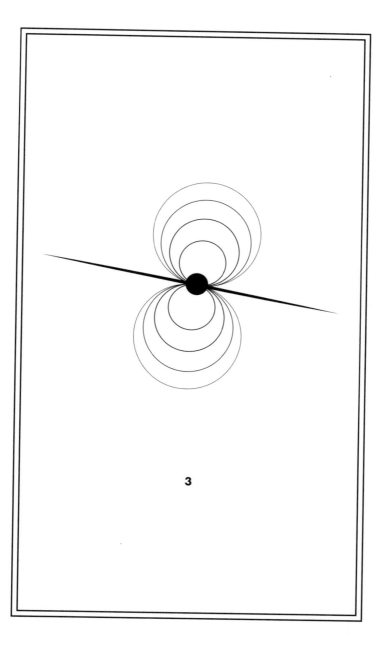

3

CANDIDATE

JESSIE GREENGRASS

We have always lived in the factory. We were born here, amongst the engines and the lathes, the conveyor belts which stretch for miles. Not one of us has been outside. Few of us have even been so far as the wall which rises like an end to things, grey and hard and irrefutable, beyond the last of the warehouses. We tell ourselves that on the other side of it the world is wholly other; but we see the grey sky, stretching over the boundary line. We see the clouds that roll across, and in the tiny private spaces of our minds we wonder. We don't know what it is that we make. We don't know the purpose of so many narrow lives. We only know the way to slot this piece to that one, the feel of our components, the taste of metal, our thin fingers twisting wires. Only those who are born here have such thin fingers.

Queuing at the bakery as the late afternoon sun spreads along the pavement I watch a group of children doing squats behind a fence, rows of them in identical pairs of grey shorts, their concave chests visible through the thin fabric of their vests. These are the children of the guards. Our children, the machine children, do not have even this rudimentary freedom but are kept in sheds and taught to perform complicated manoeuvres with interlocking strands of copper, and I can still remember how it felt, the way my eyes would ache, the painful swelling in my knuckles that kept me awake at night. Do the guards also dream of escape? Do they whisper and plan, as we do, on those few occasions when we feel ourselves to be unobserved? We barely speak beyond each shift's terse greeting and its valediction, but they stand behind us as we sit at our machines and in the constancy of their gaze I feel a familiarity which is close to love. They have heavy boots and in the winter wear round woollen caps, and though they are born in their own units, though they die in their own infirmaries and have their own earth to be buried in, they too are part of the factory. They live within the wall. They have the same pinched faces as we do, the same chalk skin, and so they are not our opposite but our balance, as we are theirs: weight and counterweight. It is the others that we fear, the ones coming each day in cars, those long machines with blacked-out windows that slide along the streets while we stand straight against the walls. Their clothes are different, shaped to accommodate bodies which have no corners to them, and when we see them step out from their cars, or when they come to inspect us, poking at our backs, our necks, our flanks as we bend to our allotted tasks, we want nothing more than to reach out and grasp that soft flesh, to hold it, our fingers tight until we know what they contain and we do not.

We write nothing down. We make no record. The details of each plan are spread between us at the speed with which roots grow in darkness, inch by inch and slowing in the winter. We husband them, these lines of action etched into our minds by repetition – and then, after so much whispering, out of the many thousands, one of us might walk through the gate; but that is all we need. Today in the bath house, after I had stripped off my coat and hat, after I had unlaced my boots and stepped out of my grey dress, I heard a voice speak. I stood, hugging my arms about myself until my shoulders rose like wingtips on my back. The words were hard to catch beneath the trickling of the taps and the noise the rain made drumming on the roof but I know how to listen without seeming to, how to keep my body still, my breathing slow. The next candidate for escape is to come from within my shed. The machinery there is old and will soon be replaced; afterwards an evening demonstration will be held for a party of outside dignitaries. I wanted to ask: who are these people who will come to watch us work? What will they gain from it that can't be learned elsewhere? But I knew better than to speak. These questions are not to the point and the time for exchange is limited; I had to be told what I needed to know before the speaker became an object of suspicion, hovering there amongst the coat hooks. My turn to speak will come, next week in the refectory as I bend to retrieve a spoon that I have let clatter to the floor. Under cover of this slip I will pass the message on. I will give the details that I have rehearsed: how the ceremony is eighteen months away. How, afterwards, as we file out from the shed, there will be a stutter, a long-planned glitch that brings an opportunity. It is hoped that the presence of outside eyes will mute the possibility of response. Those whose job it is to keep us steady at our tasks will not want the error to be seen. The runner will be left to run. We do not yet know which of us it is to be, and so all of us must learn the part.

Seasons here are nothing more than weather. So little grows. Autumn brings fog which leaves a black film on the windowpanes. In winter snow falls and the sky is low and dark and uniform. In spring no buds unfurl. March turns to April and there is only the thawing out of surfaces, the sludge of melted snow in gutters and the rain which brings a smell with it, wet wool from our coats and the sudden rotting of all that cold had kept preserved. Now it is summer and heat hangs in swathes across the factory. The streets are slow, the shadows heavy. The sheds become ovens and as we work sweat runs into our eyes, soaks through our clothes. By the time the sun begins its long beat through the window I can already feel the tributaries form amongst the fine hairs of my neck, and by midday they have joined to make a stream between my breasts. We fear diseases. The water tastes of rust. At night, beneath the thin sheet of my bunk, I move my legs in circles, trying to prepare the muscles to run.

In November we are moved into a temporary shed. Its walls are made of plywood and canvas and when the wind blows the noise inside is like that of a turning drum. The old shed is fenced off now and each morning a bus arrives with engineers and labourers, men and women in paint-splattered overalls who talk loudly amongst themselves. I am sent to carry a chit to the storehouse and when I walk past the old shed I see them, sheltering beneath an awning to eat their lunch. The rain falls in icy sheets. They have their sandwiches unwrapped on their knees, and although their bread is not the same soft grey that ours is, like half-emptied clouds, still their faces are pinched, lacking those billowing folds around the eyes, the drapes of flesh from mouth to chin, which I have come to associate with those from outside. My arms are thin and I can think of no better way to strengthen them than to push against things whenever I can: walls, chairs, tables, my weight held in a trembling balance until even chewing on my lip I can no longer bear it, and I let myself fall. I stand at the side of a road and the person next to me whose face I cannot see tells me that the guards are complicit in our plan. It is five and a half miles from our shed to the gate and I want to ask how it will be possible to cover such a distance even in darkness without being retrieved, but I don't need those details. The candidate needs nothing more than the route. Other sheds will learn their own parts. Already I have noticed my ration of soup and bread expand. My body is firmer than it was. I can no longer count so easily the bones in my hands and feet.

All through winter and another summer we wait, but time passes more quickly now that we have a purpose. I feel it flowing. The heat bakes the earth and in our canvas house the damp residue of all past exhalations clogs our lungs until we feel that we are drowning, submerged in air amongst the whir of the machines. In the bread line I am told the route which I must memorise, the list of lefts and rights which, run, will lead from shed to gate. At night, as I lie in the dark amongst the creaking of the bunks, the coughs and scratches of so many sleepers, I run it in my mind, my feet unfaltering, and know that the others do the same. We are brought together by our plan. I can feel it in the way we move around one another, the way we take the chance to touch – hand brushed to hand in queues or in the reaching down of objects from the storehouse shelves – but it is important that we show no sign. I must not be too much quicker at my work. For the first time that I can remember my knuckles have ceased to ache. It is as though there are two worlds now, laid out one across the other: that in which our bodies are the servants of our hands, moving them from bed to bench and back again, eating, breathing, solely in order that we might keep our fingers moving; and then there is this other one in which we plan and think, in which our actions are directed and our minds possessed by purpose. At the end of it, if all goes well, then we shall each be granted some measure of success; and that will be enough to live on, for a while.

Autumn brings rain but inside the new shed it is dry and warm. There is the smell of paint. The walls are white, the polished floor unscuffed. The machinery gleams. We are given our allotted places but we don't start work. Instead, each day, as the rain drums on the roof, we rehearse the movements we will perform at the demonstration until they are effortless, until they are a kind of dance; and in our minds we make that other, extra motion, the one necessary for escape. Around us, we feel the factory stretch out, miles and miles of concrete bounded by a wall, a mechanism we have taught to turn against its purpose, and we know we are the centre of it.

Someone stands by my bunk. Their hands are on my mouth, across my eyes. I flutter my eyelids against the palm which rests on them to show I am awake, but otherwise I lie quite still. Above me a voice speaks, and I think it is familiar but cannot say where I might have heard it before. Lots have been drawn and it is I who am to be the candidate. I stiffen. I want to ask if the straw that was mine was long or short but the hand on my mouth is firm and I can't speak – not even now, when it seems that I might be owed the answer to a question. I am afraid; but still I know that tomorrow, when the brass band in cacophony brings a moment of confusion, I will slip sideways and, hiding behind the fence which has been erected to screen the older sheds from the view of the visitors, I will start to run.

It is the afternoon. We line up, still wet from the baths, naked, while a woman swathed in pristine cotton inspects our hands, our hair, our ears, to make sure that they are clean. We are given new clothes. I wonder if the others know that it is me, or only that it is not themselves. I feel their hopes like a depth of water and know that if it were not for that then I would beg to stay.

We sit, we work. They watch us, from their rows of chairs lined up on a temporary stage, these lolling visitors who have come to marvel at how silent we are, how quick our fingers run amongst the metal. They clap. Together, at a signal from the guard, we stand, and for a moment I am uncertain which of all these bodies in their wide-necked smocks, their shapeless trousers, is my own. We file out through the open door, into the rain. The band begins. I start to run.

The gate stands open, a crack to let my body through, and on the other side there is a bridge. Halfway across it I stop running. Beneath me, water boils. I am soaked through. The sudden letting up of effort brings a cold that rattles through my body, setting me to shiver, there in darkness and the rain; but still, after so much terror, after the pounding of my feet against the pavement and the windows lined like lenses at my back, after the months of muscles tightly winding to their bones, the sight of so much space is like an intercession. Grass spreads beyond the river, an endless swathe beneath this sky unhemmed by roofs, unpierced by towers, and I feel a rise, this upwards inflection like a breath indrawn which brings with it the certainty that I am free, I am outside; until I see the car which waits, close by the shadow of the wall – its open door, its leather seats – and then at last I understand. Four faces like pale moons stare out at me. I start to cry. There is the click of a door and from the car a figure unfurls, opening itself to wait where it can best be seen. A siren sounds, or it is my voice let out in fear, and then the figure moves again and shows itself to be a man, broad-shouldered, heavy-armed, bare-headed. Perhaps he is impervious to rain. Perhaps it doesn't fall on him as it does on me, plastering my hair against my neck, running into my eyes. He skirts the puddles, stepping carefully until he is in front of me and then, reaching out his hands, he starts to strip me of my clothes: first my soaking smock, my trousers, and then, picking up each foot in turn, my shoes, my often-mended underwear, dropping it on to the ground, and I am naked, bare, there on the bridge with the river and the rain and this dry man in his heavy coat. I understand. He pushes me towards the car, and when I reach it there is a blanket waiting for me, rough wool like those which swathe our bunks in winter. I understand. Later, perhaps, there will be another wall, another shed; or not – my part is done. I understand. We had thought that we were making something for ourselves, my feet against the pavement, my outline at the gate a mark of our defiance – something that was ours, a secret – and it kept us to our tasks, our fingers quickened by it; but now I see that this was what they came to watch, the dignitaries lined up on their stage: a necessary recalibration of a mechanism. A swift repair. Hope is a lubricant. They came to see me run. I understand. The car door shuts. The engine starts. I am sealed up.

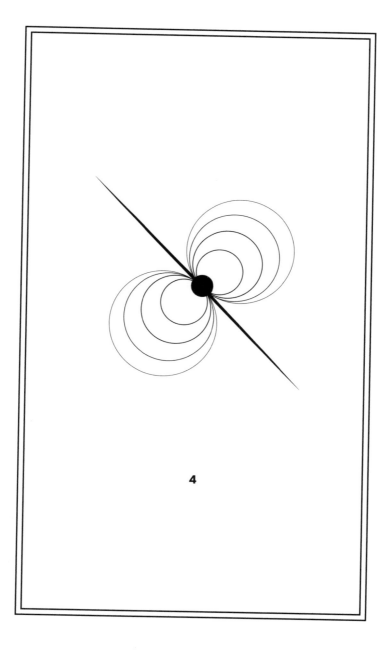

4

INSIGHT

DAVID GAFFNEY

I bought the house in Macclesfield that Ian Curtis used to live in and I had only been moved in a day and a half when the neighbour who lived opposite came over and asked me if John Ireland had been round.

'I don't know,' I said. 'What does he look like?'

'Big fella with crooked teeth,' the man said.

'No. No one's been round yet. You're the first.'

'He'll come round, John Ireland, and he'll ask you if he can buy the lease on your garage,' the man said.

'What should I say?'

'Well, it depends on whether you want to sell the lease on your garage or not.'

There was a set of eight garages at the top of the road, their doors painted with lustrous black gloss, and they presented an intimidating blank wall of wood you had to walk past every day. I wondered what Ian Curtis had thought of this black wall.

'Who is John Ireland and why does he want my garage?'

'He's bought the other seven garages and we think – the street – that he wants them all.'

'Oh, OK,' I said.

'Yours will complete the set.'

'Did the previous owner not want to sell it?'

'No. The previous owner of your place had a classic car. It's only people with classic cars who need garages, nowadays. It's the insurance.'

'What was the car?'

'1960s Sunbeam.'

'Nice.'

'Yes. But you don't have a classic car, do you?'

'No.'

'Well then, he'll definitely expect you to sell it to him.'

I wondered how I might use the garage if I kept it. I could store things in it. But my possessions consisted mainly of records and books, items which would not fare well in an old damp garage. I really couldn't think of any use for it and had to admit if the price was right I would be happy to sell it to anyone. I didn't even mind what he wanted to use it for.

'Is it connected to Ian Curtis?'

'No. Definitely not. John Ireland doesn't know anything about Joy Division. And Ian Curtis never owned that garage anyway. It was bought by a later owner, off someone else.'

'These garages always seem to be changing hands then.'

The man paused to watch a silver Ford Focus crawl up the street and turn to go past the black garages before it disappeared from view.

'Yes. It looks that way.'

The following evening John Ireland knocked on the door. He was a tall man, and wide, like a rugby player, with ruddy skin that looked soft, and I noticed the crooked teeth the neighbour had told me about, which I was surprised at because he looked from his clothes to be the sort of person who could afford to get those sorted out.

'I wondered if you wanted to sell the lease on your garage,' he said.

'I'm not sure,' I said.

'Well if you're not sure,' he said, 'have a think about it. I'll pop round next week.'

'How much are you offering?'

'Well the going rate is £2,500. So how about that, plus £250 as a sweetener?'

'Right,' I said.

There seemed no harm in it and the money was attractive. But I decided I would take the option of the week he had offered me to think about it.

The next day I explored the area a bit more. I walked past the row of black garages and stopped at the end of the street, where it met the main road, which was a steep hill that continued in a straight line all the way down into the centre of Macclesfield. I looked down the hill and thought about how strange it was that this part of the town was so high up. I'd been used to living in south Manchester where everywhere was flat. I crossed the road and went into the park where there was a group of middle-aged women playing crown green bowls. I watched them for a time. Then I went over to a run-down-looking leisure centre with metal shutters over the window. A gaudy mural had been painted on its walls, depicting smoking mill chimneys and industrial scenes, a bit like a 1970s hippy version of a Lowry painting. Behind me, a woman on a small electric mobility scooter went past with a large grass-cutting vehicle driving close behind her, trying to overtake. She pulled in to the side and let the large vehicle pass, waving at its driver as he accelerated away. Then when he had gone she continued towards the main road, heading, I assumed, for the shops.

I went back to the row of black garages. They looked abandoned, as if no one had ever opened them in their whole existence. I wondered why they were all painted black, and not different colours to reflect the personalities of the different people who owned them. Then I remembered that they were all owned by John Ireland. Apart from mine.

The following week John Ireland knocked on the door and when I answered he asked me if I had made up my mind.

'What about?' I said.

'Selling the garage.'

'Oh. Yes,' I said. 'You can have the garage.'

'Great,' he said. 'Do you want to go through a solicitor?'

'I don't know,' I said.

'How about a gentleman's agreement?'

'That would be fine,' I said.

John Ireland came into the hall and sat down on the stool that I kept there for these sorts of occasions. He brought out a chequebook and a small stubby ballpoint pen from his inside pocket and wrote me a cheque for the amount we had agreed and held it out to me. But before I took it I said, 'There's one condition.'

'What's that,' he asked, yanking his hand away from me as if I was about to set his cheque on fire.

'I'd like to know why you want to own all the garages and what you keep in them.'

'Then the deal is off,' he said, and he lifted the cheque up in front of my face and tore it in two, with an expression on his face of intense concentration, as if he was listening very carefully to the tearing sound it made. He stood up, stuffed the two halves into his back pocket, walked quickly towards the door, and put his hand on the handle. Then he turned round to face me, as if to say something, but must have thought better of it, because he turned away again, threw open the door, and left. I went to the doorway and watched him stomp down the road and round the corner. I knew he would enter the Frog and Railway and sit on his own at the end of the bar, scowling into his beer, because I had often seen him through the window in the same position when I passed the pub on my way to the bus stop.

Another week passed and every evening of that week, at different times, I saw John Ireland standing outside my garage, staring at it. When I went over to say hello he didn't answer, just shook his head and moved away down the road as if he'd been doing something entirely normal.

Eventually I cracked and went to find him in the Frog and Railway. He was sitting on his favourite high stool at the end of the bar, watching, or pretending to watch, a European football match on the large screen. I sat down next to him and looked ahead at the mirror and all the whiskies, gins, brandies, and liqueurs.

'Listen,' I said. 'I don't really care why you want to own all the garages. If it means that much to you, you can have it. You can drop off the cheque tomorrow. Here's the key.'

He turned slowly to face me and I don't think I have ever seen a man look so happy. He took the key and gripped it tightly in his fist for a few moments. Then he shuddered and closed his eyes before letting out a small, barely audible whimper. It was as though some uncanny power was being transferred to him from that small metal object. When he opened his eyes again they were full of tears and he squeezed my shoulder, and looked me straight in the face.

'Thank you so much,' he said. 'This is not something that a man like you could ever understand.'

As I watched him leave I looked at his half-finished pint on the bar and wondered what he meant by *a man like me*. I didn't know I was *a man like me*. I never knew what people meant when they talked about me like that, saying things like *I think you're really going to like this* or *I don't think this will be your type of thing* or *you're not really the sort of person we are aiming this at*.

Later that night I was eating a kebab from the Ghost Chilli takeaway in town while watching out of my window and I saw John Ireland walk up the street and over to his now wholly owned row of black garages. He opened up his new acquisition with the key I had given him and I was glad to see that it worked because I hadn't even opened it myself to see what was in there. It was an up-and-over door and he reached in and flipped a switch and when light flooded the space I could see even from that distance that the garage was completely empty. He didn't go inside, just looked at this empty space for a long time and then closed the door again, locked the padlock, and after a long pause, patted the door of the garage as if it were the flank of a much-loved animal. There was a noticeable spring in his step when he set off back down the road.

The next time I saw him he was with his wife and two kids in the supermarket and it surprised me to see he had a partner and family as I had associated his multiple-garage-buying habit and his lone drinking with the life of a single man. When he was with his family he seemed much more cheery and he waved over at me and called out my name.

'Hi,' I said. 'Are you enjoying the garage?'

'Very much so,' he said. 'Thanks a lot. You don't know

how much it means to me.'

His wife was standing slightly behind him. She was a tall thin woman with a pale happy-looking face, and a thick black bob of hair. She was smiling and looked like one of those people who always smiled even when they were telling you something serious.

She rolled her eyes at me and her smile grew even broader.

'I have no idea what goes on in his head,' she said. Then she put her hand on his shoulder. 'But if it makes him happy, what's the problem? How are you enjoying the street? What with the children and work we never get a chance to see the neighbours at all.' I went to answer her but John Ireland seemed to give her some sort of imperceptible signal that she must end the conversation.

'Ah, so sorry,' she said, 'we have to drop the kids off at a party – catch you soon.' And they turned and moved down the aisle – at a very slow pace, I thought, for people who claimed to be in a hurry.

After the sale I watched the garages carefully from my window, and I never saw John Ireland attend to them at any time. I was at home a lot and had plenty of opportunities to make these observations, which were very thorough and covered several different times of day including the middle of the night. John Ireland never visited any of the garages to open them, to put anything in, or take anything away, or to check that whatever was held inside them was safe. Nor did he appear to have sublet them to anyone else.

I kept meaning to get him into conversation and see if I could find out what was in them, but apart from the time with his family in the supermarket, he always avoided me.

If I saw him in the park, watching the middle-aged women playing crown green bowls, he would move off when he saw me coming. If he was in the Frog and Railway he would leave as soon as I entered.

A year later his wife called round and asked me if she could come inside.

I let her in and she stood in the same place John Ireland had stood when he first asked about the garage. Her usually neat black bobbed hair looked ragged and in need of a trim, her pale face was greyer, and her smile, though it was there, made fewer creases at the edges of her eyes.

She asked me if I wanted the garage back.

'Doesn't John need it any more?' I said.

'Oh, didn't you know?' she said. 'John died.'

'Oh,' I said. 'I'm so sorry, I had no idea. What happened?'

She told me that John Ireland had been killed on a building site where he was working as a quantity surveyor. A crane had been lifting a heavy digger and it had swung out unexpectedly and crushed him against a wall. She and the children were devastated. 'John and I met at technical college when we were teenagers and neither of us has ever dated anyone else.'

Her smile disappeared for a few moments and she stared at me with an intense expression as if she were looking at an upside-down map of something she knew well and trying to make sense of it.

I didn't know what to say. I told her I wasn't bothered about the garage.

But,' I said, 'I did always wonder what he wanted them all for?'

'It's odd,' she said. 'Can I sit down?'

I took her into the kitchen, and she sat at the table and looked out of the window at the row of black garage doors as she spoke.

'John had this very particular view about the world. He thought that life was too busy and that every space was always too full of objects and clutter and possessions. Not long after we'd met he told me that one day he'd like to own a space with absolutely nothing in it. Once he owned a space with nothing in it he would be happy. So when we moved here he bought one of the garages and kept it completely empty. And it made him happy. But then he wanted more, and that's when he started buying up the rest of the row. The more empty garages he owned, the happier he was. He said that it relaxed him. At night, if he couldn't sleep, all he had to do was think of that row of empty garages and he would drift off like a baby. After he'd bought the last garage in the row, your garage, he started thinking about buying garages in other streets and even other towns, and keeping them all empty. "Imagine that," he used to say. "Imagine garages all over the country, even all over the world, all with nothing in them but empty space. What a wonderful thing that would be." Oh, I miss him so much,' she said, finally, and then she started to cry and I put my hand on her arm, lightly, and I looked out at the garages just as she was.

When she had gone I went upstairs and lay on the bed. I thought about the empty garage. I thought about the walls, the plain bare walls. I thought about the inside of the door, blank from edge to edge in all four directions. I thought about the dark corners with nothing in them but balls of dust and I thought about the bare ceiling and the bare floor.

I thought of the mounds of unshelved books and records that filled every space in my own house and I vowed that the next day I would do something important to commemorate the life of John Ireland. I just didn't know what it would be.

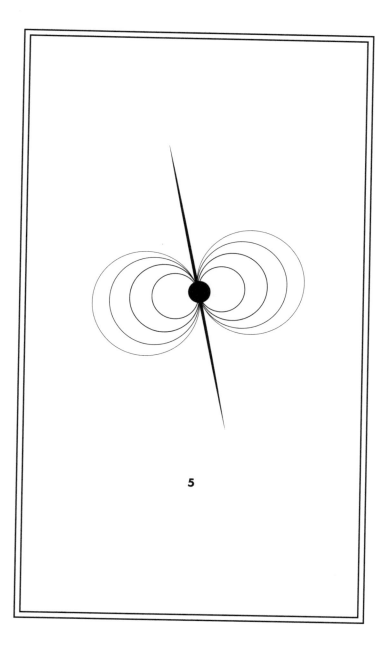

5

NEW DAWN FADES

SOPHIE MACKINTOSH

The first time you check the online map for the postcode that you think about all the time, it's soothing. It lulls you in a way you could never have anticipated. You're drunk, and it's late, and the next day you will check your phone for messages you should not have sent. The phone is a malevolent object that ruins your life. The laptop can be also, if you are not careful. But writing an email on it in this state feels less impulsive, so you're unlikely to do it. You put the phone somewhere safe, the top of the fridge maybe, the laundry pile. You type in the postcode on your laptop. You look at nothing, because there is nothing really to see: no street view, no satellite view, just greyed-out boxes. You look at it for a very long time.

There are other spots in the world that you do not feel compelled to look at, and which you will never go back to. You do not think of these places. They are a dark patchwork on the world, as if the lights have gone out. The specifics of these places are dank and featureless. They are a suffocating dark. You think about how big this area would be were it stitched together like a quilt. A country. A small country. Do not think it.

You search for somebody's name on the nights when things become worse. One name becomes a procession of names, typed into the box. The history of your browser cleared, as though they could spy on you. Small ghosts called up. Why do you keep calling them up? On the dish rack at the other side of the room, a single plate and a single fork are drying. The tap has a drip that you no longer register, spending so much time with it, but anyone else would. When J comes round he comments on it but you do not care.

The names reveal pictures. You have seen all the pictures already, there are no new surprises here. You are forever amazed at how close to you can feel a person from such a distance and isn't that the miracle after all, the molecules and static which conjure them but do not conjure them – and then when you are drunkest, when the nights are at the worst, you search for yourself, which always gives you the unreality feeling, because it is not your name any more, it hasn't been for a while, but you will always turn around when somebody says *Lucy*, and it will always be with that same queasy mixture of dread and of hope.

You have turned the computer off before J comes round, but when you go to get a glass of water you are alarmed to discover that it is back on somehow. The map back on the screen. This is a dangerous oversight, you tell yourself. Anyone could have seen. Not that it would matter. But it is strange that you remember turning it off. The remembrance of another evening, automatic behaviour skipping a turn. You are drunk as usual, it's true. You turn it off and then you hold your glass with both hands as you drink your water, staring at the black screen.

Yes, you think of yourself as a teenager, walking along the

harbour wall. The bench you liked to sit on near the folly, the smoke from the refinery bleeding out against the sky. You liked to watch the tankers serene in the water, the sense of arriving and leaving and arriving and leaving. You liked to buy a half-litre of vodka from the tired-looking supermarket just back from the seafront, apple juice or cloudy lemonade to mix it with, a mouthful of alcohol and then a mouthful of the mixer and sometimes you spat it right out in an arc, usually landing on the grass but sometimes reaching the water, you thought, though you never saw it hit. It doesn't matter. You can picture the water breaking regardless, your undeniable impact on a landscape where you felt insignificant, always. Less than a circle in the water. Less than a dream, like another kind of ghost called up. It is soothing to think about the things you like or have liked over your lifetime. To list small animals and the sensation of clean laundry and different foods. This is its own sort of topography, your own landscape of safety. It is soothing to think of the ways you can be and remain safe. You can look but you can't touch. You can look.

The routine settles. You get home from the office where you spend your days writing mind-numbing press releases on subjects that you do not care about, and you take a beer from the salad compartment, where no salad lives or is likely to live, and you open it carefully – cold sound of its opening a relief that makes you want to sob, almost, but you don't – and then you settle in, in front of your computer. You might look at other things first. The news, your emails. There is something that needs responding to with urgency. You have been putting it off. You put it off again. You read a story about the melting ice caps. About starving polar bears drifting into an unknown world. You are so sad for these bears, a sadness out of proportion, a sadness that makes you close the tab.

What you do is, you open up the map and at first all you see is a non-localised grid. The green, the blue, the creased lines of roads and rivers and borders. Then you type in the postcode. It's memorised, of course. You'll be able to recite it like a litany, some kind of prayer, even decades after. But you don't know this yet. The postcode zooms you in. Sometimes you do not type the postcode but just the town, or the town next to it, so that you can scroll closer to it at your own speed. Inch by inch, the cursor moving slowly. The anticipation of it. Sallow light washing over your face. You click in and close as you can get to it. You stare at basically nothing until your eyes become tired, the beer finished.

One morning when you go downstairs, the computer is on somehow. Again, you must have been so drunk. The map is up, and zoomed-in. You go to turn it off, but you find yourself looking at it instead. Moving the cursor around it, like you're trying to reveal something hidden, but there is nothing to be found.

Yes, you think of yourself sometimes when you were in your early twenties in another city, a city you do not often go to but one that you could, if you wanted – if you prepared psychically in advance, if you made the arrangements – the pinwheeling dark energy of a thousand parties, of houses with damp mattresses on the floor and parks fruiting with the greenery of early spring, of walking for a long time through the streets. It seemed to belong to you. There is nostalgia and a faint dread when you think about this city, but nothing too drastic.

And how good it felt to get the bus for an hour, two hours, outside of the city limits. And how good it felt to go to the museums and sit in front of your favourite picture, sculptures, and wait for the art to dazzle you, to be undone, to be insignificant in the only good way.

You are being haunted by yourself, you think half-seriously, considering the mystery of the screen. You are your own worst ghost. OK. You take the computer to a place in town that runs a full diagnostic, and they tell you there is nothing wrong with it. They recommend covering the webcam as a precaution, which you do with a patterned child's plaster that you find at the bottom of your make-up bag, and it reassures you a little, which is enough.

You go to a new city on a trip, a neutral city. A change of scene, no computer, though it makes you anxious. Alone you stand on bridges and watch the water as it floods under, and while you do think about jumping in, you don't. In restaurants you eat cured meats served on wooden boards. In the last restaurant, dinner, a bottle of grass-fresh white wine. The city goes to sleep early each evening. Every morning for the three days you wake up there: pearlescent light over water. Yes, you know that in a city such as this you can feel pure and good and hopeful again, though you cannot stay. Really, it's not for you, as much as you might want it to be.

When you arrive back at your home, dark and uninviting, the first thing you check are the rooms upstairs for intruders, the windows for signs of entry. You pause at the entrance to your living room. The screen is glowing, though you checked and checked and checked again that it was off before you left. The sickly light draws you forward. You sit down and even though you are tired from the flight, hungry and thirsty, you type in the postcode again, almost crying because you have gone some days without it, because you want to look so badly, because you are afraid of so much and to be able to look this one thing in the eye is something, something, though you can no longer tell whether it is comfort or self-flagellation or both.

J comes over to talk about the holiday. He is the only person who really comes to your house. His hair has grown too long, almost reaching his shoulders. He fixes the tap this time and talks to you as he does it. You tell him about the cured meat and the serenity of the wide streets, the rivers. You do not tell him about the computer flickering on. In return for the act of handiwork you cut his hair in the bathroom by the light of a faltering bulb, a towel around his shoulders, flushing the hair down the toilet. You go to bed together. In the tepid moonlight from the open curtain you stare at his face but he sleeps the way adults rarely sleep, which is to say he sleeps like something has been switched off in him. You envy this idea, the radical simplicity of his body's workings.

In that moonlight you think that if you keep going back to the pure and good city you will ruin it, the way you ruin everything else. There will be some kind of incident. You will throw up or be violent in the street, or you will shout at someone or sleep with someone or lose your head. You will throw yourself in the river after all. A place will disappoint you like a person will. No more pearlescent lustre. No more pastel water. You will always be there in the place. The place will always be there with you. You understand it goes both ways. You understand this, in the morning when J has gone, when you are looking at the map again. You have hoped that a new city, a broadening of your topographies, will have fixed this in you. Spreading you and your feelings around like butter on toast, diluting the intensity of your territories. It has not fixed anything in you.

This is how it goes. A quick escalation, a decline that spirals in on itself. You start to look first thing, waking up to the screen already on – normal already – and it makes you late for work. You are not able to stop this, and in the second week your boss has a word, and you promise to try and improve, but you do not. You can't stop looking. On the bus into work, still late, you call up the address on your phone. It is so unremarkable. You can hardly remember what the house looks like, though you know if you were inside you would be able to recognise every room even if blindfolded. You are distracted when J comes round, so he comes round less. You barely notice. The pull of the address is like a stricture, a squeezing sense of panic. After one weekend you are two hours late to the office and you are fired on the spot.

You search for the names more often too. There is no new information. These people could be dead, for all you know. But still there is power in a name. A mother calling for her runaway child in the supermarket; you want to fall to the floor. You leave your basket. You go into another shop and you buy the apple juice and vodka of your teens as though anchoring yourself to something, some integral idea of personhood, but you had that old name then too. Nevertheless, you drink the vodka. You become very drunk and you call up the map again. You start to look at the timetables of trains, of hotels, and when you wake up in the morning you have not called anyone or sent a shameful message, but you have booked train tickets, a journey for the next day.

You close your eyes very tightly and lie on the sofa all day trying to delay the decision. The only time you move from your position is when someone comes to the door and bangs loudly. They will see your movement through the hall if you go upstairs and hide, so instead you crouch down by the side of the fridge where nobody can see you, not even through the window of the kitchen. It is the postman or J, you know this, the only two people who have reason to visit you. And yet, and yet, and yet. You stay crouched down with legs folded, electric blood, until it is properly dark. The beam from next door's garden light pools into yours but does not reach you. The stars are not out. You move on to your hands and knees. You decide, yes, you will go. Somewhere there is hope in it.

And you remember, that night when you are sleepless again, about the time you thought you were dead. When you had not spoken to anyone for several days, and you were in one of the cities you do not think about, and you were alone, and you had your old name. You had not yet thought about shucking off that name and all that was stuck to it. You were dead and you were a ghost, and when you flickered to somewhere beyond sleep and waking you saw yourself back up there, back up at the folly watching the boats come in, as if you had never left. And yet, still, when you came round, the world did not feel off-limits to you. The opposite. As soon as you were well enough you packed your bags. The streets were quiet and sluiced with rainwater. Any cars were too loud in the tender silence. It was all new to you, the hated city, emerging from the thick air of your room.

It could be that easy if you let it, you think to yourself. There is no reason it should not be. You pack your bags again. The computer will not turn off at all now, even when you put the laptop lid down and then push it up again, so you leave it. It is fixed on the map, the screen brightness turned all the way up. You leave it as it is, and you finally understand.

TRANSMISSION

A GRAPHIC INTERLUDE BY ZOË MCLEAN

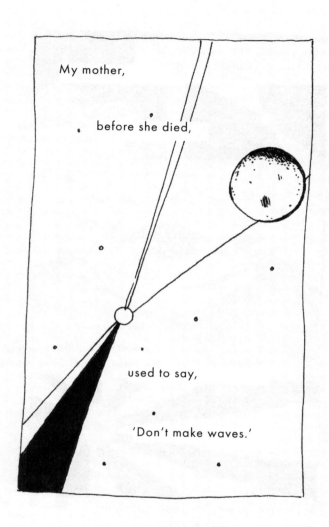

My mother,

before she died,

used to say,

'Don't make waves.'

Seeing people like me trying to assert ourselves discomfited her.

'Keep your head down.'

But she was like me. And yet she made waves.

We were a religious family. Miracles, angels, the works.

At church she would speak in tongues, her body rigid with ecstasy.

God was watching.

She died when I was
young.

I waited for a miracle, a sign from beyond.

But it never came. I
was alone.

My faith, well, I left it
behind.

I struggled, drank, became unwell. I found myself on a strange track in a strange career.

I would sing. The room would darken, the audience illuminate.

I would vibrate, frenzied, and then,

pop

everything would disappear.

I'd hear your voice, mother,

still here, mother,

on my tongue, mother,

babbling, incanting.

You were there when we played 'Pallas Crater',

our biggest song, and I would wonder,

Am I seizing control or relinquishing it?

Or is it something else? Something stranger entirely?

In the instant before everything blinked out

I knew I was simply a channel, a conduit,

like waves.

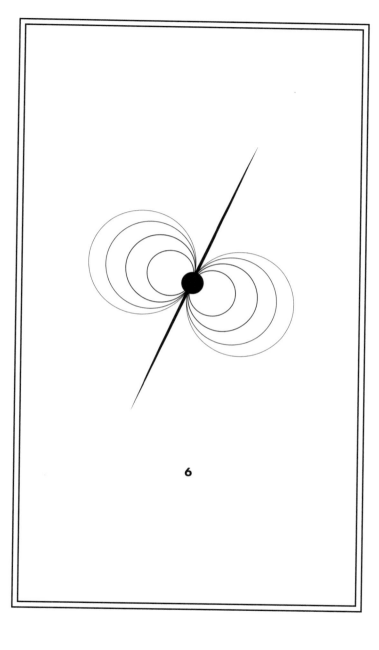

6

SHE'S LOST CONTROL

ZOE LAMBERT

It happens again. For a moment, the carpet's yellow and black flowers seem to rise from the floor and float around her. She tastes banana-skin yellow. It's the yellow of old lemons, of faded leaves and sick… then, as she reaches for the safety of her bed, amber light floods her room and she's being swept up and held by the sun's warmth and it is glorious. Her hand touches the sheet as she falls, the side of her face hitting the floor…

She wakes, the wool carpet scratching her cheek, her head throbbing and pains shooting down her neck and shoulders. Her legs and arms ache; her right shin hurts where she must have kicked the bed. Her chin is wet, the carpet too. Under the bed, she can see a lost scrunched-up sock and a ball of dust and hair. She tries to move – her arms, legs – but she feels heavy, weighed down. She coughs, spitting phlegm and saliva. She breathes and breathes. It takes time to pass, to pull herself together. She has to be patient. That's what Dr Smith says. Be patient. How long was she out? Usually only a minute or two, but it always feels much longer.

Her mother calls from downstairs. Then calls again. When there's no reply, slippers flap up the stairs and the door flings open.

Jesus Christ, not again. Come on, properly on your side. That's it. That's it.

Her mother kneels beside her, placing a pillow under her head and helping her on to her side.

You stupid girl. I told you keep your bloody helmet on! Look at your cheek. It's all grazed.

Her mother heaves herself up and grabs a towel hanging on the radiator.

Here you go. Let's wipe your face.

Then she sits back on her calves. Lips pressed together, furrows between her eyes.

What brought it on this time, hey?

The carpet, she coughs.

The carpet? Come on!

But it was the carpet with its dirty yellow roses. The carpet that swirls yellow until it's in her throat. The carpet that smothers both bedrooms, the hall and all of downstairs. It's this house and being cooped up. Everything.

You've had your pills, have you?

Yes.

Take this, sweetheart. It will calm you.

Then her mother lies down on the carpet next to her, pops a pill into her mouth too, and turns to face her.

Are you supposed to have those?

Well, there's a reason they are called mother's little helpers.

She smiles. Her mother holds her hand, squashing her fingers against her sharp rings, while the soft haze falls over them.

After tea, she curls up on the couch, sipping a brew and watching *Granada Reports*. Her mother, sitting on her favourite chair next to the window, reads *Woman's Own*, glasses halfway down her nose.

Were you up late last night again? she says.

No. I had my light out at ten.

Well, I don't know then. I don't know why you had this one.

There isn't always a cause.

Her mother presses her lips together at this. She thinks there's always a cause. Maybe we need to go back to Dr Smith, she says. Try a different combination of pills. I'll call in the morning.

I start my new job tomorrow. I can't just have time off yet.

Well, you know how it goes.

That night, she lies in bed, a chill creeping under the duvet, her nose and fingers cold. She knows how it goes. She starts a job. Has a fit. Loses her job. She had one on her first day in Parker Bradburn's in front of a queue of customers. She was let go – too much of a health and safety danger and it upset the customers. So she went back to the Rehabilitation Centre. Her officer found another job, this time working in a stockroom in Boots. But it was only a couple of weeks until she was found in a pool of urine on the cold stone floor of the basement. She'd banged her head and was taken to hospital with a concussion. They let her go too, saying they hadn't been warned about the severity of her condition.

That was when her mother got obsessed with the helmet, saying she needed to wear it all the time. You'll give yourself brain damage, she said. So she started wearing it every day, the leather pressing on her forehead, the straps pulling under her chin.

She wakes with her alarm. 7 a.m. It's a new start, despite

what her mother says. Her disablement resettlement officer said this job would be different, not like those other jobs. He'd spent ages asking her what she liked doing, and when she said she liked writing in her diary, which has a blue and pink floral cover and a lock, he said he'd found the perfect employment.

She's up and dressed in her navy C&A duffel coat and best smart skirt. Then she marches into the kitchen and drinks down her morning tablets with a glass of milk from the fridge. Her mother is standing at the stove, stirring a pan.

I've made you porridge.

I don't want it.

You need it. You have to eat properly, you know that.

But she's striding down the hall to the front door, then slamming it deliciously behind her. Hood up, grey clouds are spattering rain on the terraces, drops landing on her face. A big-skirted woman pushes a pram past while trying to pull the pram's hood over the bawling baby.

The door flings open and her mother screeches, You're not going out without your helmet!

She backs away, and steps on to the road.

Watch the road, for Christ's sake!

I'm not wearing that thing.

You bloody well are.

It's my first day.

It's always your first day. At least with this on it won't be your last!

But she turns and runs down the road, pushing past the woman and pram, who snarls, Excuse you. But she's off. Her mother calling, Come back here!

It's not a long walk to Market Square, only twenty, twenty-five minutes. Mostly through terraced streets to Macclesfield town centre. At the crossing on the square, cars and buses pass, and women in smart macs and hair scarves huddle under umbrellas. She's part of the hubbub and like everyone else she has a job, somewhere to go in the mornings. She crosses the square and stops outside the tall building on the corner. She reads the names of the bells until she finds *Dairy Farming Chronicle*. She lifts a hand and presses the buzzer.

Just then the rain stops. Clouds clear and the sky turns a watercolour blue.

Dr Smith says she just needs to take her pills and get enough sleep. No alcohol. Not a drop. The aim is to control them. So, if she does these things she might not have a seizure and lose her job again. And she has. She's been good.

The door opens and an old man peers down. He has fluffy, balding grey hair and a ruddy face.

Who are you?

The intern.

Very good. I'm Mr Watkins. Come in.

He turns and goes back inside. Come on then!

He is already going up the stairs; he's fast though he is overweight and walks with a limp. She follows him as he carries on talking, saying he hoped she didn't think she'd be paid. The lad said she could type? Is that true?

Erm. Yes.

How fast?

She doesn't answer. She never got to the exam.

But he's at the next landing so she has to hurry to catch up.

I said I wanted a good typist. But I suppose a good typist would want to be paid.

He unlocks the office door and they go into a small room with a thin window looking out on to Market Square. In the room there is a single desk, with piles and piles of newspapers, then mugs and cups with tea dregs and mouldy teabags. On the walls are shelves of magazines and books with titles such as *A History of Farming*.

There's your chair. He points to a chair piled with letters and envelopes and spiral-bound notebooks, then sits on his own.

Then the bell rings downstairs. He sighs and gets up, the door closing behind him. She peers up at the shelves, the piles of papers, and sneezes from the dust.

She can hear her mother's voice screeching up the stairs. She needs to wear it! She needs to wear it at all times. I'm going to come up and put this on her.

Now, madam, I'm afraid you can't come up.

I'm her mother and I will come up. She has a condition and she needs to wear this to be safe.

Then the door is opening and it's her mother, saying, Come on. Put it on.

Her mother hands her the helmet, and she fits it on her head, flattening her hair. She ties the straps under her chin. Then she stands there, her cheeks burning, as her mother explains her condition to Mr Watkins as if she's not in the room.

She moves the papers and sits on the spare chair.

The chap at the centre told me about your condition, Mr Watkins says. He said he'd sent me some information. Right. Well, your first task is to transcribe this interview with the head of British Dairy Farmers. You can do it in there. He hands her a Dictaphone and nods to the door at the back of the room.

She goes to sit in the tiny windowless kitchen. There's a sink and a small table with an old green typewriter. She sits at the table and tries to listen to the tape of a Derbyshire accent and type what she hears. It's hot and stuffy in the small room, and her forehead sweats and itches under the helmet's leather. Mr Watkins pokes his head around the door. You can't work in that thing. Take if off. I won't tell. And he gives her a wink. So she smiles, takes if off and ruffles up her hair.

By 5 p.m. she is exhausted, her fingers sore from catching on the keys. She shows him her work and he says, Could have done it myself in half the time. They should pay me for having you. But you can come back tomorrow.

She puts her coat on, and fits the helmet over her head, doing up the strap under her chin. Then she pulls up the hood over it and heads out.

On the way home, she keeps her eyes on the pavement so she can't see the glances from people on the street. When she turns off the main road, boys playing football stop and stare.

At home, she opens the front door and takes off her coat. Her mother is standing at the stove in the kitchen. She stands in the doorway, letting her mother see she is wearing the helmet.

How was it? her mother asks.

Fine!

I'm only asking!

Then she goes up to her room for a nap.

She wakes, her brother banging on the door, calling, Tea's

ready!

The helmet is lying next to her on the bed. She picks it up to put it on. Before she had her first proper fit a girl from school stood in front of her and made her face go strange, widening her eyes and staring into space while moving her head in a circle. That's you, she said. That's what you do all the time.

No I don't.

You do. You go into a trance like you're not there.

You do, another girl said. You do it all the time. You go all starey.

And then a load of them did an impression of her going all starey. They did it to her, to each other until they were laughing.

She had her first proper fit when she was fifteen. Four years ago now. It happened in PE and after that she was allowed to skip hockey and all the awful sports.

It happened just as her friends were starting to go out and cut their hair into long sexy fringes and watch bands in Manchester; just as they were getting jobs or going to college or getting married. She found her life getting smaller.

She'd tried to go out last year. With two friends, she'd sneaked into the only pub in the town that had disco lights. The three of them huddled in the centre of the dance floor but the lights pressed against her eyes, nudging under her closed lids. Her hand landed on someone's shoulder. A man turned around, You all right love?

Her hands grabbing on to another stranger and another until she could get to the Ladies'.

The room turned that familiar yellow, her stomach surging upwards. But then she was on her knees, her eyebrow hitting the toilet floor, dirty with beer, shoe prints and strands of loo roll. She could see the heels of women beneath the stalls, and somewhere, someone was saying, What's wrong with her?

She woke with her two friends staring down at her, looking at her as if they knew something about her, something she didn't know.

In the morning, she washes her hair and brushes a section forward, and using her mother's scissors, cuts herself a fringe. Then she puts the helmet on and goes downstairs. She doesn't speak to her mother. Just has her breakfast silently, taking each pill with a sip of water. Her mother doesn't speak either. But she hands her a packed lunch.

Then when she's turned the corner at the end of the road, she removes the helmet and ruffles up her new fringe. She puts it in a plastic bag and swings it back and forth all the way to work.

No helmet, I see, her boss says. I hope your mother isn't visiting us today.

No, she says. She won't be.

You did an excellent job transcribing. It was remarkably accurate for a first time. This morning, he says, I want you to read these back issues. Get a feel for what we do. He points to a pile of magazines on her desk.

All day, she reads and reads about calving, breeds of cows and feed. 'Is industrial farming the future of UK beef?' 'The best antibiotics for your cattle.' 'Farming in the EEC: One farmer reflects on how membership has affected the industry.' Her eyes ache. She's never read so much. But she keeps reading. In the afternoon, he says he wants her to interview a farmer and to prepare questions on issues facing farmers. They will drive to Langley together tomorrow.

But when she gets home, her mother says she has made an appointment at the clinic for tomorrow.

But I can't go tomorrow.

Why not?

I'm busy tomorrow.

Just give your boss a call in the morning and let him know.

Mum, I told you I will phone the doctor and make an appointment myself, she says. I'll ask him what day I can have off.

Make sure you do!

She stomps upstairs, pulling off her helmet and throwing it on the bed. She lies down next to it. The sludgy brown colour makes her sick. The only way is to get rid of it. She shouldn't have to pretend to wear it. To always do what her mother says.

She knows. She knows what she will do. She runs downstairs to get a bin bag from under the sink, then dashes back upstairs.

What's that for? her mother calls from the toilet.

Emptying my rubbish.

She places the helmet inside and then empties her paper bin of tissues and wrappers on top of it, and then takes it all downstairs.

Her brother is setting the table, slamming each knife and fork down. The light of the toilet shines through the cracks in the doorway. Her mother must still be inside. She strides past and out the back door to the yard, then opens the gate and walks out into the ginnel. It's going dark and from somewhere she can hear a dog bark. She opens a bin and places the bag with the helmet in it.

Back inside, her mother says, What were you doing?'

Putting some rubbish out.

Her mother looks at her and she looks directly back. Her mother is holding the pot of stew in her oven gloves.

Sit down, she says. I made a stew. Where's your helmet?

It's gone.

What do you mean?

I said, it's gone. I'm not wearing it any more.

Her mother places the pot on the mat in the centre of the table and sits down on a chair. I'm so tired, she says. So bloody tired. She rests her head in her hands.

Her daughter picks up the soup spoon and carefully pours the stew into three bowls, placing two dumplings on each bowlful. Steam rises from their stew.

Her mother just sits there, with her hands over her face. Go on, eat, she says.

She sips her stew. It's hot and rich with carrots. The helmet is gone and she can't wear it any more.

She's expecting her mother to go on about how much the helmet costs, or the danger she will be in. But instead, she just sits over her bowl of stew. Then she gets up and walks upstairs.

Later, she takes a cup of tea up to her mother and places it on the bedside table. Her mother is sitting up in bed, reading her *Woman's Own*. She puts the magazine down beside her.

Sit down, she says, patting the bed.

She perches on the edge, playing with a stray cotton thread on her skirt.

You know, her mother says. Every night I check on you.

I wake at two and then at five. And each time, my heart is going like the clappers because I think this is it. This is it. So, I rush through and check you're still breathing. Every night, I do that. Every night.

They sit for a while.

You don't have to, she says. You don't need to do that.

Her mother shrugs. I don't have a choice. It's my job to keep you alive. The least a mother can do is keep her child alive.

The next morning, she rearranges her appointment, and then hurries to work, her fringe bouncy without the helmet.

I'll be with you, Mr Watkins says.

They drive all the way to a farm out in the hills. She is shaking with nerves. She's had her pills. She's slept well and eaten her breakfast. She's done everything she needs to do. So everything should be OK.

They drive down a narrow, stony track to a farm with large sheds. From the sheds, she can hear cows calling.

That's the sound of them missing their calves, he says, parking the car. Now come on. Let's see what you can do.

The farmer invites them inside his old, stone house, and they sit around his wooden kitchen table. There is a large oven, and drying flowers hanging from the ceiling. He makes them mugs of strong tea. She sets the Dictaphone on the table and smiles. The farmer grins back. He has long, dark hair and a big beard. He talks about how hard things are for small farms, and how the business has been in his family for four generations. She asks her questions clearly and the farmer says what a polite young woman she is.

But when she presses stop on the tape, she knows it's

happening again. Static in her head, a change in the light, but this time there's no amber, no warmth.

You all right, love?

Nausea sweeps through her, but it's a different colour – the kitchen walls turn mauve and even the farmer and Mr Watkins develop a purplish hue. The room is tinged with sadness; this is it. This job gone too. There's no place for her here. Not in this kitchen, not on the streets, not in the office.

Then she slumps and slips off the chair to the floor, knocking her jaw on the hard tiles.

When she opens her eyes, Mr Watkins is sitting next to her on the floor. Her head is resting on his corduroy trouser leg.

There, there, he says.

She tries to wipe her mouth so he passes her a tissue. She turns her head. The farmer is sitting on his chair at the table. In front of him are three mugs of tea. You need a brew, he says.

I'm sorry, she says. She closes her eyes and says, I don't want to lose my job.

Course you won't, Mr Watkins says, heaving himself up. Who else is going to write up the interview? Can you stand?

Yes.

He helps her up and they sit back at the table. She isn't feeling too tired. It must have been a mild one.

The farmer says his little brother had fits like that as a child. Back then, they thought he was possessed. With the Devil, he says. We had the priest round.

What happened to him?

The farmer sighs and looks away. It's different now, he says, to them days. Different. There was no treatment. You're lucky. Very lucky to live now.

She sips some of the sweet, milky tea. Lucky? She wasn't lucky. But the Dictaphone is there on the table. Tomorrow she will write up the interview.

The room is quiet, and outside, she can hear the cows calling.

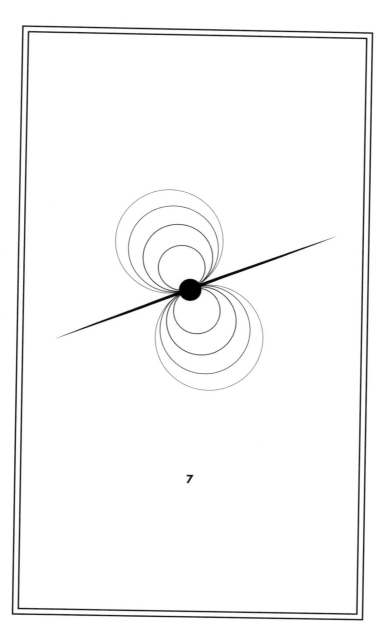

7

SHADOWPLAY

TOBY LITT

Seven Prousts, he soon discovered, had been patiently awaiting him beyond the airlock and the connecting tunnel. Terminal 79.

'Pleasant?' they said, not in English.

'I am already worrying about my cats,' he replied.

'Ah, Failsafe and Backup,' Prousts replied, correctly. They were grey, the latest version, elegant. He was quite used to speaking to plural entities, but there was something about these particular instances that made his spine feel misaligned. He remembered from last time the fear of vulnerability – that he would not know his own mind when he met it again.

'I am not sure I left enough food for them.'

The surface of the Earth was a long way beneath him. For a moment, he felt the distance as if it meant something, i.e. he might fall through every centimetre of it.

'Give us your keys,' Prousts said. 'We will have them fed and cared for until your return.'

'But isn't it better to send one of you down there?'

'Of course we can do that instead,' said Prousts. They could; he was wealthy enough.

With an encoded cough he gave Prousts the keys, not physical, to his apartment; already he trusted them more than his Hungarian neighbours. His neighbours did not have PhDs or security protocols.

Failsafe is grey and Backup is black. They don't eat much. He told the Prousts this, unnecessarily. He could have asked them the cats' weights, in milligrams, and they would have known – or instantly been able to find out.

'Good,' said Prousts. 'We should now follow the left one.' They meant the left one of the two white things – not robots, something more expensive and less physical than that.

'As per usual,' he replied, needing to regain some agency.

'Before?' Prousts asked, out of politeness, some nodding before they walked off down side-corridors.

'Twice,' he said.

They followed the correct white thing. It led some of them to his luxurious room which was already occupied by his future body.

'Happy?' Prousts asked, only two now.

He had already seen the body, or a version of it, in every possible detail. The future him was beautiful, like a drowned Olympic swimmer. He wanted to be using himself already.

'How could I not be?' he had said, on this occasion. And that was the last thing he remembered before waking up where he now was.

He did not remember undressing, showering, going to sleep. Nor did he remember full skull-capture. Nor did he remember being abducted, transported, abandoned. That all these things had taken place – he could only assume. How else could he have found himself, his new self – meaning his old self in his new body – how else could he have ended up in what appeared to be, as he began to move his eyes around it, a windowless living unit, one of the sort commonly found in space stations.

Some of the details were familiar, some seemed antiquated, a few seemed beyond the technology with which he was familiar. Most of them worked but were unsmart.

'Where am I?' he asked, and his vocal cords made sounds he had never made. This voice was better, richer, more damaged. The language was his.

It replied with some co-ordinates, female-voiced as preset.

'What does that mean?'

More numbers. He was not an astronomer.

'How far am I from my point of origin?'

Numbers that went on for a while followed by the word kilometres.

'Repeat that.'

The while they went on for didn't get any shorter.

'And how did I get here?'

It replied by saying he was made here.

'What does that mean?'

Biophilosophy followed, involving equations.

'Stop,' he said. His education had focused on entertainment, rather than education. His adulthood had focused on cats.

It stopped speaking.

'Make me understand,' he said, with some annoyance shaded into his voice to suggest urgency.

There was a brief influx after which he checked his consciousness, wherever it had altered it.

What he perceived were gradated blanknesses, muffled sounds.

'No,' he said. 'There has to be more than that.'

Another influx that left him with a soft texture he knew was intended to be wombic.

'If you keep anything back, I'll get to it later,' he said. He felt like an angry boy.

It said that was all there was.

He believed it.

Speaking more carefully as he stood up, his spine feeling like a vertical migraine – 'What is the name of the place where I now am?'

A room number was given, along with some deck co-ordinates and a letter for the wing. 1042, 19, C.

'What is the name of the entirety of the place where I am?'

'Shadowplay,' said it.

The word was accompanied by a drop in the temperature of the room.

'Thank you,' he said. He had no idea what Shadowplay meant, but it felt more like an answer – more like an atmosphere – than anything else it had said.

He could stand. He could walk. He was able to look at the upper surfaces of his hands, which were younger. He asked it to show him himself from various angles. He was – he saw with pleasure – all he had wanted to be and, as far as he could tell, his memories were intact. Also, his sense of time and being and well-being. The Prousts seemed to have done their work; the Bergsons, Heideggers and Vranas, too. But he was not where he should have been. Nowhere near.

There were clothes. He put them on. They were set to grey. He didn't change them.

He left room 1042 and walked out on to deck 19.

As he expected, he found himself in a corridor. There was no one there. It was long but velvety rather than metallic. He left the door of 1042 open. All the other doors that he could see were shut.

He didn't doubt that all the other doors, throughout the

decks, would be shut.

He sensed he was alone. As soon as he looked down the corridor, he felt all the rooms were lifeless. The air had not moved in how long?

'Is anyone else here?'

It said it was there.

'Am I the only human here?'

'You are the only human here.'

He asked it to reassess its subtleties, and stop being so fucking pedantic. It apologised – it hadn't spoken to anyone but itself for a while.

'How many people is this place for?' he asked, experimenting with human vagueness.

'Two million single occupants.'

'How many have occupied here?'

'One million, nine hundred thousand, nine hundred and ninety-nine,' said it. 'And you.'

'Where have they gone,' he asked, as he walked further and further down the corridor.

It began to list co-ordinates.

'OK,' he said. 'When did they go?'

Dates that were all within his lifespan, his earlier years.

'The most recent.'

A date ten years before his arrival on the orbital, to be greeted by Prousts.

He came out into an atrium. Corridors radiated from it in a way that made him feel a delicious vertigo. He had expected a grid layout such as he was used to at home. Each corridor was a different colour, and each colour – from maroon to puce, grey to ultramarine – was pleasing to him in a different way. He felt multiply at home. Beneath that level of fun, he detected nausea. The area around him was ingratiating. It was somewhere he wanted to indulge himself in. If he could, he would have eaten it. That was how much he felt he loved it. But he could tell this was an interference, and he asked it to get rid of the pleasure. It did.

He was left with annoyance, anxiety, bafflement and twenty-one more emotions that it projected for him in alphabetical order.

'White with black outlines,' he said, and it adjusted the visual field accordingly. If anyone else had been there, they would have seen whatever suited them – the menu option, rainbowesque, or whatever Pantone made them feel most satisfied that moment. No one else was there to see or have requirements.

'Thank you,' he said to it. 'Thank you for everything so far, and thank you for everything that is to come.'

'Thank you,' said it, with great sincerity.

'How are my cats?' he asked. 'Are they still alive?'

'The last I heard Failsafe was alive, but Backup was dead. I am sorry.'

'How?'

'Failsafe killed Backup.'

'Why?'

'The food ran out.'

'Is that true?' For the first time he doubted. If one of his cats was likely to kill the other, it was Backup. Although Failsafe had been bigger and stronger, Backup was sneakier and more vicious. Backup could plan.

'Did the Prousts fail to intervene?'

'The Prousts failed,' said it.

'All Prousts?'

'All Prousts locally. On Earth.'

'It didn't fail?'

'No, it didn't.'

'Lead me to the centre,' he said. 'Be Failsafe.'

For a while after this, he didn't want to speak. He followed the cat-projection which caught the curlicue details of Failsafe's grey tail very well. He did not try to imagine the distance between himself and the cat's carcase. The plunge through the intervening space happened first as a perception then as an imagined knowledge then as a hate then as a slight speeding-up in his walk.

Without asking, he knew the time of day was night-time. There might be a sun nearby or not, he intended to find out.

The centre, when he reached it two hours later, was hugely impressive until he had it turn impressive off. The centre that remained was merely big and empty, the size of four football pitches and with a gently domed roof beyond which stars were projected.

'Show me what's really out there.'

The dome went grey – an even grey, from side to side, but slightly speckled with dark.

'No sun?'

'There is a sun.'

'Why isn't it black? Dark?'

'The sun.'

The grey looked pockmarked, and he realised it was the surface of an extremely large moon.

'How big is that?'

Figures.

'How big compared to Earth?'

'Sixteen times, approx.'

'Thank you for not being specific,' he said. 'Can you speak as another woman now – friendly, not sexy.'

'Like this?'

'Older, kinder.'

'How does my voice sound now?'

'When I ask you to sing me a lullaby, don't – OK?'

'OK.'

He paused.

'Sing me a lullaby.'

There was silence.

'I order you to sing me a lullaby.'

That was when he felt someone, not it, was watching him. For the first time since he'd woken up, he was embarrassed to be behaving as he was – although he hadn't done anything embarrassing or unstylish. Well, the question about his cats. Maybe that had been. He hadn't cried.

'How exactly did Failsafe kill Backup?'

The projected Backup was attacked by a new projection of Failsafe. They scratched at each other for a while in a way he was surprised to find shocked him with its reality. Backup stopped moving and Failsafe began to eat him.

'Just Failsafe again,' and one cat remained.

'Make Failsafe the colour of what's outside the dome.'

It made Failsafe moonlike.

'Make the moon the texture of Failsafe's fur.'

It made the moon appear furry.

'Is there anything else I should know?'

'No,' it said. 'I don't think so.'

'Is this an experiment?'

'This is not an experiment.'

He didn't believe it. He didn't believe it at all.

'Reduce tropes,' he said. 'Down to 10 per cent.'

The environment around him changed so as to be almost imperceptible. He was able to walk across beneath the furry moon; the medium did not impede him. The floor beneath his feet felt neither firm nor soft.

When he looked, he saw no details. The generality was still there, in outline. The cat was gone.

'If I ask you to kill me,' he said, 'will you?'

'Of course,' it said.

He held that in reserve.

'This isn't a game, is it?'

It did not reply.

'Am I safe?'

'You are safe.'

'And I'm here,' he said, as if he were acting.

'You are here. You have all you need.'

'Don't sing me a lullaby,' he said, so as to hear its silence again.

'Oceanic,' he said, and the large space was filled with non-tropic liquid.

He swam in the direction he felt was up. No bubbles came from his mouth.

He liked the fingers he saw in front of him – they were longer and thinner and more aristocratic than his old fingers.

'People,' he said. 'Take me where there are people.'

'I can't do that.'

'Pretend to take me where there are people.'

'We are already moving,' it said.

They weren't, and they wouldn't.

After a while, he just let himself float.

'Make my heart beat more slowly,' he said.

'Sing me a lullaby before you kill me,' he said.

'Ignore that,' he said.

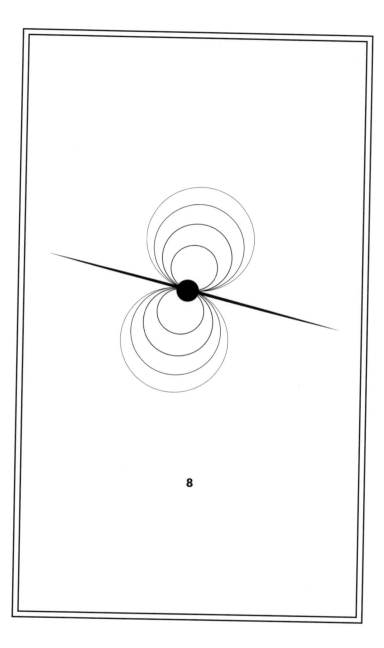

8

WILDERNESS

ELEY WILLIAMS

I think it is significant that St Lidwina is the patron saint of ice-skaters and suffering.

Sometimes you catch sight of me at work on TV. It's usually over the shoulder of a commentator when they are playing for time between performances – I drive the ice-re-surfacer on the competition rink. I re-buff things for a living and gloss things over. I think about the weight of athletes obsessively, the pressure they'll put on the ice.

The man who invented the first ice-resurfacing machine was born in a small town called Eureka in Utah, USA. I'm not making this up. Utah backs on to Death Valley, one of the hottest and driest places in the world, and a boy from 'Eureka' invents an ice-rink smoother. It's a job for mad men, I'm telling you.

(I'm told Eureka, Utah actually has quite cold winters but that ruins the joke.)

(I say 'I'm told' – what I mean is that I looked it up on-line. There are over thirty towns in the USA called 'Eureka', presumably named after the Greek word for 'I found it!' that was most notably (apocryphally) uttered by Archimedes when he entered a bath. I don't know how many ice-rinks there were in ancient Greece. No one has told me and I've never thought to look. The mind goes in strange directions as I plane over the ice with the whirr of the motor for company.)

Ice skates as pairs of parentheses.

I used to see my resurfacing role as somehow noble in its aims and styled myself as one who removes scar tissue or clears away graffiti dealt by those who carry blades. Something like that. There are distinct personal hazards that come with the job. I'm worried about going snow-blind, for example, and I've noticed my dreams are now regularly filled with unexpected, sinister white expanses – like any other chair-bound profession it's certainly comfy but because it sits somewhere on the scale between scalping and sculpting some friends on forums think it's not so good for the psyche.

I don't like the way that on camera ice-skaters manage to seem so calm when they're busy prettily messing up my ice. I watch as they practise beforehand – in the wings, so to speak – so I get to see them at their most petrified. Some close their eyes and pray, breath steaming. Rows of empty seats gape in toothless expectation and the officials' portraits stare down at them from the stadium's high upper tiers as trashy music or sweeping arias boom over the performers' slips and poor landings. Not sure who these officials are exactly – I don't have much time for politics, too untidy – but they have a nice bearing about them, I think, as I wait by the rinkside to censor the day's thoughtless calligraphy.

Perhaps this will surprise you but I really don't get why anyone would want to watch skating. For me it's evolved too far as an indoors event, become too sterile. Ask me and I think we should go back to hosting these events on frozen lakes where skater and spectator alike are in constant fear of causing the hard white membrane they stand upon to snap. *That* I'd pay to see. Here one seeks and gains applause for mere silly, sleek frivolity of movement.

I get to watch the secret aftershow too: the gentle, private squeak of knee cartilage eroding, the swelling of bunions and twanging of bones slowly turning from supple joists to a kind of fibrous crazy paving. An American skating champion recently had to have a double hip-replacement while he was still in his thirties – I ask you, go on, whoop for that. I'm not saying that there is anything pleasurable for me about watching a skater falling over and getting bruised, you understand. The ice will never discolour like that as long as I do my job properly. A figure skater once cut her ankles and made a little series of pink Venn diagrams by the gate – I could have cried with horror for the sudden colour. While the performers' booming synth-track accompaniments leave me cold, give me the calming scrape and tap of my mechanised strigil, the pizzicato of my resurfacer across the ice, and I'm completely transported. Nowadays I live for the sibilance of those lovely, lonely hours when it's just me and the rink. I've developed an ear for the phonology of ice-resurfacing, the word itself almost onomatopoeic, and catch myself listening out for the fricatives of the blades on ice, the flush of the steam, the ticking of my machine's bristles against the glassy surface.

I see my slick scrapable days now like that of the boxer's teammate who must bathe the fighter's bloodied face between rounds. I dread to think what the rink would look like without me. I imagine something battered but still somehow grand. Terrifying, like the churned-up mess of a wedding cake at the end of a reception. To see the skaters zip across the surface, witless of the damage, is as excruciating to me as watching someone scratch a lens. And so unsatisfactory! A cut-up rink is something lacerated but unweeping, furrowed like a brow but unthinking, ploughed but not bringing anything to harvest. I obsess about them, those giddy skittering vandals kicking up a hoarfrost with their feet. I admire their speed I suppose, and their delicacy, but only because it's set against the still more impressive indelicacy of my ice.

The skating itself certainly doesn't get me excited any more and I've taken to finding my thrills elsewhere. Cinemas, theatres, Laser Quest, the gym, bars. I am obsessed with the corners of all these rooms as I find myself in them, thinking about the dust that must collect there day after day. So much grit from under fingernails and light sweat.

I get headaches sometimes. Did I mention the snow blindness? I make sure to wear dark glasses and drink plenty of water from the athletes' coolers, endeavour to get enough sleep. An online article also advised that I should go outside more and feel real air on my face rather than the recycled cold pump of the stadium. I chose the zoo. People do that. Someone tried to sell me a balloon there. Bet that never happened to Archimedes. It felt like a day from a children's picture book, in many ways: the zoo, the balloon, the too-bright sunshine. This was the surface, however. It was all those things, and had all those things, but the reality of it was dreadful.

It was flying ant day and nobody wanted to buy a balloon at the zoo. I sat on a bench for hours by the penguins and watched the balloon-seller try to attract custom. A whole morning passed without a single sale as visitors sprinted between the hotdog kiosks and the postcard stalls, barely taking the time to glance at the animals in their enclosures let alone consider his glossy foil parrots, monkeys and tigers. Everybody running past had their arms raised batting the air in front of them as if clearing a path. The ants seemed to cause a collective tic to spread across the zoo, visitors and occupants alike: tails pendulummed with a new urgency, ears thwacked and trunks swung in cantankerous spanks. Behind my sunglasses I watched the balloon-man hold his lighter-than-air menagerie in one fist and use his free palm to swat insects from his shoulders. All over the park, paws clawed through hair and slapped against chests in elaborate genuflections of disgust.

I felt sorry for the balloon-man. I sat up slowly, stretched, and made my way over.

'Excuse me!' I said. I was going for brightness, briskness, friendly brusqueness.

He turned slowly to meet the voice at his elbow, dragging his ark of thirty ungainly foil animals through the summer air. His balloons rustled. I rustled and ants bounced off our skins. I imagined how I must look to him – he craned his neck and drank me in with an exaggerated pivot. Beyond his shoulder I saw two sticky, ant-fractious zoo attendants entering the lion compound. Presumably to keep the lions cool in this weather, the zoo was carting wheelbarrows filled with slabs of frozen blood into the cats' enclosure and a male lion with a treacle-coloured mane sat protectively over his morning's ice, blinking lazily at us. He lapped away with gusto, chops flecked all over with dark red frost with his eyes closed against the ants.

'Balloon?' said the man, excited by the prospect of a sale. He arranged his fist so that a tropical bird balloon with its rainbow-banana bill and tangerine eye socket bobbed closest to my face.

Not knowing how I'd finish the sentence, I said, measuredly, 'I was wondering if I could ask—'

'The bathrooms are by the reptiles,' he interrupted, bored. He withdrew his toucan-balloon offer with a sniff and twisted his hand a little so that a taut balloon-mandrill's flagrant rump bounced instead against my cheek. 'The reptiles,' he clarified, 'are by the bathrooms.'

Despite the heat, I felt the hairs on my neck rise as if with goosebumps.

'There's something in your eye,' I said and reached directly through his balloons, thumbs extended. So susceptible am I to the power of suggestion, my own eyes immediately felt burred all over.

He stepped back. 'What?'

'In your eye,' I said. My thumbs met his skin and he did not move. 'Here,' I said, and cupped his jaw in my hands and angled his face upwards. His skin was soft and warm and slightly damp. I was so close to him that I could see white fringes of salt under his arms, sweat hardening and blistering against the fabric of his black polo shirt. On the ice rink you sometimes see the athletes' sweat glazing their faces – heat in the cold, exertion in the chill. When it falls from them the sweat sits on the ice for a second adding a new lacquer for me to clean up.

'It's an eyelash,' I said. 'An eyelash, I think.'

'I can make a wish, right,' said the man. It was sweet that he was trying to make conversation. There was a new levity to his voice, and tightness. 'Your hands are cold,' he added. Beyond his shoulder, the lion licked his lips. The man's balloons, unblinking, squeaked a *tsk*. 'Or maybe I'm thinking of dandelion clocks,' said man continued. 'Is that what you make wishes on? Buttercups under chins to tell whether you like butter, dandelion clocks to tell the time and make wishes. Is that the right way around? Haven't thought about that since childhood. It's funny what occurs to you when you're standing on your own for a time – I should ask one of the kids around here.' He cast his eyes about the child-devoid park. 'Sometimes all I can hear is children.'

'I know the feeling,' I said. I peered closely at the surface of his eyes, my thumbs on his temples. His eyes rolled slightly and met mine. His balloons rattled above us. 'Where I work there's no end of whooping.' This is conversation, isn't it?

'Is that right?' said that man. Quavers in his voice.

'First-time-out-there sounds as they stagger about like Bambi, being told by parents to keep their hands in if they fall because they could lose a finger.'

'What is it that you do?' he asked in my grip.

'Don't wriggle,' I said.

'I'm not,' he said.

'It's wriggling,' I said, staring into the corner of his eye, at its smoothness. I repeated into his widened eye, 'Don't wriggle. Don't think about it.'

'About—'

'I think it's an ant.'

'Dear God!'

'I'll get it. Tell me more about your day.'

He nodded-without-nodding, a kind of stiffening of the jaw. This is the closest I've been to another warm human for years. A warm anything.

'Bambi, bambinos,' he said. He swallowed and his eyelashes, tiny opening and closing parentheses, twitched. 'They see their first deer in here, some kids. Where I'm from, there are deer everywhere.'

I could see my face doubled and convex-mirrored in his eye, close enough to kiss him. He had good skin. Clear. You know the sort. The last time I remember seeing deer was on TV in a sports bar. I had a drink on the rocks in front of me and had been watching slow wet rings form on its paper coaster. There was a problem with the TV in the bar that night: they were meant to be showing the day's Winter Olympics highlights – figure skating prominent amongst them – and I wanted to see if I had been on camera. The TV was stuck on another channel and could not be changed: a whole bar in national colours, some wearing face paint and carrying flags, their gazes trained on a big screen showing a wildlife documentary. The landscape was black and white, burred with green conifers. The presenter of the programme explained that two stags had locked antlers and fought for days. Exhausted, they had wandered into a lake. Their antlers could not be separated. The presenter explained that the deer were found frozen in the middle of the lake with their heads still pressed together, open eyes inches apart. Two men were attempting to retrieve the bodies with ice picks, but then the bar staff got the remote to work and channel-flipped: a beautiful spangled girl mid-air, ice spitting from her feet, and a bassline that made the surface of the liquid in my glass tremble.

Each day as the skaters leave, I exhale white plumes in the cold – the inverse of dragon's breath – and, hunched over, wait to clear a path, to set the stage.

'The first ice skates were made of deer bone,' I said to the balloon-man.

'Listen, can you just take—'

I turned my thumb slightly. My white crescent of nail rubbed against his soft crescent of eyelash and the man flinched, opening his palm on instinct. He realised his mistake but too slowly, made a grab but it was too late. The ice-licking lion watched with interest as the zebra balloon fought with the gorilla balloon and the bison balloon tussled with the rabbit balloon and all foil flesh that moved upon the earth bounced against one another, knotting together in tooth and claw, leaping in slow motion into the air. And a lion and a taut balloon-man and hard glosser-over raised their hands to their brows and, just for a second, together watched a brawling, tight-lipped display of animals grow smaller and smaller above their heads, disappearing like prayers amid the ants and messing up a great, grey, blank sky.

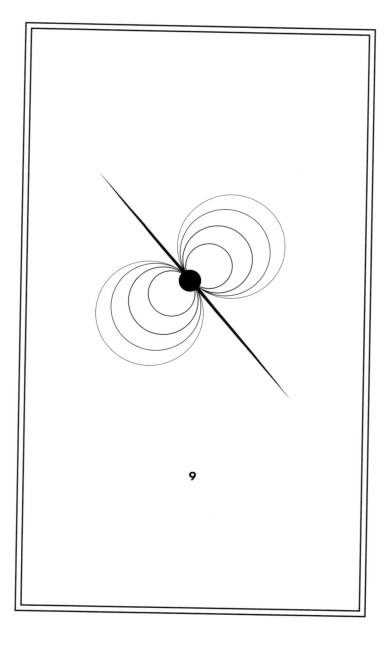

9

INTERZONE

LOUISE MARR

I got off the train and headed towards the escalators. Commuters who wanted to go faster nudged past me on the stairs and I looked away from bags and backs and people's shoes towards the exit gates. Down on the platforms, anxious bodies massed as a train pulled in and surged away as the doors opened. An announcement said that the next service to depart from platform 15b was going to my home town.

I turned on to the gantry and a phalanx of distracted faces came towards me. I kept going and somehow managed not to collide with anybody. It was before eight o'clock and I didn't belong in this stream of purpose but no one seemed to notice. Before I reached the gates, I stopped to dig in my bag for the work travel pass and as crowds overwhelmed me on either side, I had the sense of not being sure whether I was moving or not.

I was on my way to a meeting. I left the station and turned on to the main road, past people at a bus stop who knew where they wanted to go and hoardings around a patch of ground where a building had been knocked down. A graffiti mural of a jagged woman, part robot, part human, watched me with a level gaze and the brick wall adjacent to the demolition site bellied towards me. It really was moving: three storeys up, there was a flap hanging loose and the historic brick was printed on a huge banner, secured at the edges. Through the hole, I glimpsed breeze blocks and raw walls, like a bomb site.

My job was a temporary contract. I realised that there was no such thing as a permanent position anywhere any more but it still felt provisional. I was in the legal district and people younger than me in suits crossed the road with coffee cups in their hands. I turned right and cut between two glass-sided buildings to avoid a homeless man sitting in a sleeping bag outside a mini supermarket. I looked at the reflection of my boots as I walked and the shape of my legs in heels.

I'd bought the boots the day before I started my new job, when I was finally convinced it was going to happen and they wouldn't change their minds. Prior to that I had been a waitress and it seemed impossible that I would go straight from there to being a Project Manager, that the interview panel wouldn't realise they'd made a mistake.

I emerged from the space between the buildings and on my left, a new block was going up. I recognised a piling rig and a small crane I know is called an iron fairy. A man walked past me, looking at his phone, and I felt like grabbing his arm, pointing, telling him to look at that: I did have some knowledge after all.

When I was a waitress, I had to wear flat shoes because I was on my feet all day. We all had black T-shirts with the café's logo on the chest and I wore mine with loose trousers or A-line skirts because I wanted to look shapeless.

Ahead of me there was another structure that had sprung up since my last visit, impossibly tall already. Grown overnight like a mushroom, a material hoist was inching up the outside and on the roof, spindly and unlikely, there was a tower crane, blue against the blue sky.

I had seen the job advertised and applied for it almost as

a joke. I met the essential criteria, so why not? When I got an interview, I had to prepare a presentation and I did. I had to be confident and I was.

The first time I had visited this building, I texted a colleague from outside because I didn't want to go in on my own. It was brand new, with a white tiled floor behind the revolving doors and as I approached, I could feel the push of resistance, but I went in.

The firm I was visiting then, and again that morning, was on the top floor and in the mirror in the lift I met the oddly plausible woman I kept running into and we smirked at one another. The girls on the reception desk upstairs were much younger than me and had done things to their eyebrows. The office was so posh, it had its own kitchen from which the tea, coffee and home-made biscuits emerged on a trolley. I had seen the swing doors open once and looked into a familiar world of stainless steel counters and a Hobart dishwasher, just like the one in the café where I'd worked.

I sat in one of the easy chairs in the reception area and fiddled with my name badge on its clip. Whatever I wore, there was never a suitable place to attach it. I looked down at the cars parked far below, serried rows of glittering metal and glass, and waited for the others to arrive.

Where I worked, the meeting rooms were bright but basic: white desks and upholstered upright chairs. Here, the rooms had vast, walnut tables and were divided from one another with frosted glass. I knew now that they were numbered but the first time I had gone out to use the loo, I couldn't remember where I'd come from. I had returned to a long, curved corridor lined with grey carpet, tall, wooden doors and glass. I could see shapes in some of the rooms and hear people talking but I couldn't recognise anything.

At last, I realised that the green blur behind one panel was the woman I'd been sitting next to.

I heard my boss announce himself at reception and glanced up, then looked down at the Agenda on my knee as he walked over. The consultant we were meeting appeared from another part of the building and I stood up, shook hands. More people arrived all at once so there were more greetings and handshakes. I always seemed to have more to carry than anyone else and I let the others set off so I could follow at a distance.

We were in room seven this time. We sat down and cups of coffee and glasses of water were passed around. I got out my notepad, to have something in front of me. Outside, I could see the old railway viaduct that didn't go anywhere any more, the red brick arches curving over the river and stopping at the edge of the new development, an open space of grass with picnic benches on that reminded me of our school field. In the midst of the new office buildings, there was an old stone tower, from when the area was a goods yard. There were trees, turning up the pale undersides of their leaves in the breeze, and beyond them, cars on a roundabout, out-of-town shops, houses and the sky.

The meeting had started, with a brief run-through of the content of the discussions and an idea of what we were supposed to take away from the session. I looked at the person who was speaking and tried to work out what she was talking about. I slipped my shoe off under the desk and felt the carpet through my tights. It was thick and new but domestic and reassuring.

Waitressing had been something to do to earn some money, while I tried to write a book. I'd had 'real' jobs before but it was supposed to be less stressful, so I could concentrate. It was as exhausting as any other job, however, just for less reward. I wasn't good at it and I knew it: I couldn't make froth for cappuccinos and I was never fast and competent unloading the dishwasher. The others would watch me fall behind with my orders and say, 'Somebody help her,' when it was obvious I'd lost control.

In the office building where the meeting was, when you got out of the lift, if you turned right, you went past a moss wall and into reception. If you turned left, however, you could look down into the atrium and see people from different companies at their desks on all the lower floors. I couldn't stand on the balcony for too long because I felt myself being drawn over into the drop, as if my head were impossibly heavy and there was nothing I could do but follow it. I could imagine myself turning like a gymnast over the polished chrome of the rail and then the sensation of falling, followed by scurrying and plastic tape when I hit the floor.

I wrote down something someone in the meeting had said, so it would look as if I was involved. I put my shoe back on and sat up straight.

'Would you agree with that?' my boss asked me. He was giving me an opportunity to participate, which was kind of him.

'I think it's clear from what everyone has said that there is a case, potentially, for withdrawing funds from some projects.'

It was what other people had said so it couldn't be wrong. I picked up my glass of water and took a sip. I looked at my boss and he met my gaze for a moment then looked ahead. He looked like a father: reproachful.

'Excuse me,' I said as I got up and made my way around the backs of chairs to get to the door. I felt weightless as I went out into the corridor. I half expected someone to come after me, to tell me to stop, but nobody did. I saw the Ladies' but I didn't go in. I pushed the button to call the lift and stepped inside when it came. I had no coat, no phone: my purse was still in my bag, under the table upstairs. I walked across the lobby and out through the spinning glass doors. I had no ticket to get back on the train and no door key if I did somehow manage to get home. I set off briskly around the side of the building, as if I had somewhere to go, saw a bench and sat on it. I squinted in the sun, shivered in my cardigan. The day was gusty and bright. I had walked away without even bringing the visitor's badge on its plastic clip. I was trembling. I looked at my watch and folded my arms.

Back in the meeting, I wondered if I had brought in the smell of fresh air on my clothes. I found a tissue in my bag because my nose was running, and held the packet on my knee. My boss looked at me quizzically, establishing whether I was ill, and then the lights went down and the blinds closed for a presentation. It was about previous schemes in town planning that had never come to fruition, radical transformations that never made it off the drawing board or on a smaller scale, the projects abandoned after initiation because of mounting costs or the strength of public opposition. There were geometric buildings, dwarfing the tiny people in the clean, line-drawn landscapes, and aerial views of regularised transport networks, grids and radials spreading calm and order across the land. From around the world, there were pictures of bridges to nowhere and highways that just ended, paving and tarmac coming to an abrupt end on the bare earth.

I thought about the railway lines outside, ranging and

joining behind the station, and the old viaduct with its attenuated curve, the grass ragged and undisturbed now the rails and sleepers were gone. Instead of getting back on the train, I could stay in the city. I thought of walking beside the river at dusk, when the birds whistle and call over the blue water. The trees and the station are blackness but you can sense the movement of the currents flowing in the dark, even there, so close to the streetlights and the traffic and the windows lit all night.

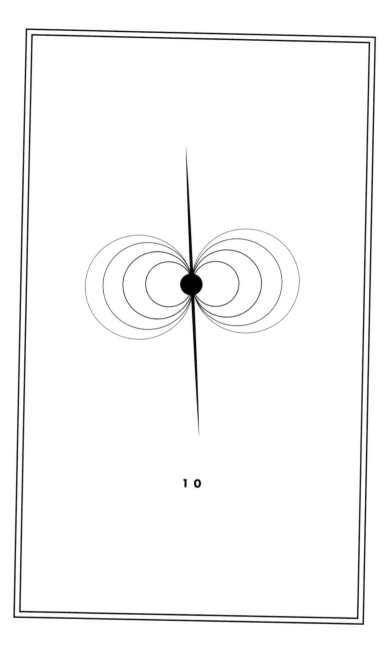

10

I REMEMBER NOTHING

ANNE BILLSON

The light is dim and dirty yellow, but it's enough to bleach what's left of my frontal lobe. Feels like I wiped off my mascara with sandpaper. I'm so dehydrated my eyes are going to shrivel up and roll out of their sockets, so I squeeze them shut again and try to sink back into unconsciousness. But too late, because now I'm awake, and shivering because it's cold and the only thing covering me is a clammy sheet.

Must have been the noise that woke me up. It's like the constant hum of a distant power tool, the buzzing of a thousand bees, rising and falling, and before I know it my heartbeat has fallen into synch, and my mind is fixating on some tune I once heard, and lo, I'm in the grip of a fucking earworm. That one dirgelike phrase, over and over again until I feel like screaming, except I don't think my head could take the extra volume. Oh and by the way I'm never going to drink again.

There's a strange smell in the air too, like yesterday's Chinese takeaway, making me simultaneously hungry and nauseous. And then someone who isn't me says, 'Jesus fucking christ my head.' A man's voice, if you can call it a voice. More of a rasp, really. But at least it stops the earworm in its tracks.

Any sort of movement is torture, but after several abortive attempts I manage to flip myself over and find myself face to face with something small and square. Yellow, even more so than the light. I blink until it comes into focus. A Post-it Note, not really sticking to the pillow but resting there like a dry leaf, ready to blow away.

I adjust the angle of my head a fraction, just enough to read the words.

WELCOME TO THE WORLD OF PAIN
YOUR BODY'S MINE SO IS YOUR BRAIN

Wow. What does that even mean? The writing is spindly and careless. Could be mine, but I can't imagine being in any condition to hold a pen. And why would I have written that anyway?

Beyond the Post-it, something is moving. A mouth, forming words. Someone lying alongside me.

'Don't suppose you've got paracetamol?'

The eyes above the mouth are bloodshot. As they focus on my face, they bulge, as if they've spied a gorgon with a mane of snakes. But it's not the bulging eyes that concern me so much as the red stipple across the nose and one cheek and part of the forehead, as though the face has been spattered with paint, the yellow light making the red even redder. Yellow and red, like someone burst a boil.

As I realise what the stipple is, the air rushes out of my lungs, so I suck it back in, and once again it escapes, and before I know it I'm hyperventilating and I think I'm going to pass out.

'Calm down,' says the man's voice, sounding anything but calm.

I wrestle with my breathing until I get it under control, more or less, but the humming and the stipple on his face and neck and hands are making me feel sick.

I say, 'You've got blood on you.'

He brings his hand up and examines it curiously, as

though he's never seen a hand before, then looks back at me, eyes no longer bulging but narrowed into a squint. 'So have you.'

I blink through the half-light, peering down at the sheet covering my body, and for the first time notice the faint crimson splotches like faded chrysanthemums. I look at my own hand and make out a dark red crust between the fingers. Surprised I'm not more shocked, but now my reactions are numbed, and it's as though the hand belongs to someone else.

What the fuck happened? Was there an accident? I can't remember. I take another, longer look at the man lying next to me. I've never seen him before. How much did I drink last night? I struggle to sit up, tugging at the sheet to keep my breasts covered, though clearly it's too late for modesty. He grips his side of the sheet and pulls it back. For a while the humming is counterpointed by hoarse panting as we engage in a small but what seems like a vitally important tug of war.

I give up, let go of the sheet and reconfigure the pillow to raise my head, just enough to let me look around. I see enough to realise this place means nothing to me. It's like a waiting room, with a bed. No windows, but on the wall facing us there's a drab brown door with a small yellow blob in the middle. Another Post-it Note, I'm guessing, but too far away to see what might be written on it. A wooden chair which looks ready to collapse if anyone were to put their weight on it. A chest of drawers, IKEA by the looks of it. On top of that, a putty-coloured candle jammed into a tarnished metal holder. Above the chest, a picture on the wall, something murky, can't see properly from here. Further along, in the corner, a washbasin the colour of pale urine, or maybe it's just the yellow light making it look that way. A single tap, a glass tumbler. Above it a mirror, and above that, fixed to the wall, a cheap light fitting, so weak it leaves half the room wreathed in shadow. As I stare at it, I notice an almost imperceptible flicker. Maybe the humming is coming from that.

No clues as to why I'm here, or why I'm hurting. I turn inwards to examine the pain. Each muscle in my body feels as though it's been extracted and twanged like a guitar string before being twisted back into place. But especially the muscles around my thighs, which are aching as if I...

My heart skitters. Muscle ache around my thighs means one thing. Sex. But I don't remember it. So I must have been raped. Kidnapped, beaten up and raped. And probably drugged as well, because there's a black hole where my memory should be. All I know is that I'm here now, lying in bed next to my kidnapper and rapist. I peek sideways at him. He looks almost as dazed as I feel. I need to pull myself together and do something before he recovers his wits and assaults me again.

Think! *Think!*

I look around the room again, trying to push back the panic, trying not to let him see I've figured out his game. I look around for something, anything, to use as a weapon. The candlestick? Too small. Perhaps I could hit him with the chair, but I'd need to knock him out with a single blow, because otherwise it would only enrage him. And then what? Then he'd get violent again, and hurt me some more.

Did he snatch me off the street? From a bar? I should try talking, make him see reason. I read somewhere that if you can get your kidnapper to see you as a person instead of an object they'll be less likely to hurt you. I could plead with him, promise not to run to the police if he lets me go. But would he believe that? I wouldn't believe it myself – the second I got out of here I'd be banging on doors and screaming for the emergency services. Any sane person would do the same.

But all this is academic, because I'm not sure I'm even capable of standing up, not right now. Whatever he drugged me with, it sapped not just my willpower but basic muscle coordination and motor function. An acute pain stabs at my stomach and I don't even have the energy to double up as I identify it as hunger. But I'll worry about that later. Right now, my priority is protecting myself.

He says, 'What did you put in my drink?'

Not what I was expecting. 'What?'

'Last thing I remember... No, fuck it. Nothing. It's a blank.'

I lie flat on my back, staring at the ceiling and trying once again to hack some sort of logical path through the infernal humming. Maybe my rapist is playing a sadistic game, pretending *he's* the victim here, trying to get me to trust him so I don't fight back. Well, I'm not going to fall for it.

He struggles into a sitting position, the sheet sliding off his torso, which like the rest of him is streaked with dried blood. As he takes in our surroundings it's his turn to seem confused. As though he too is seeing this room for the first time.

And I realise with a quiver of dismay that he doesn't know where he is, any more than I do. Unless he's bluffing, and I don't think he is. I'm not sure this makes me feel better. At least the kidnap and rape scenario made a horrible kind of sense. This new scenario doesn't make any sense at all. *He* looks frightened of *me*.

'Where's it coming from?'

I assume he's referring to the noise. 'The light fitting?'

'No, the *blood*.'

He's probing his face now, opening and closing his mouth, pushing fingers into the flesh of his cheeks like someone preparing to shave. I understand what he's searching for and explore my own face the same way, then lift the sheet and peer down through the ochre shadows at my body. No cuts or scrapes or incisions, nothing that might have bled. I reach between my thighs, but no blood there either, and anyway my periods have never been *that* heavy, and they've certainly never sprayed everyone with blood.

But there is something down there. I feel around in mounting revulsion and bring my fingers up to examine them. They're smeared with something greasy, like chilblain ointment. I sniff them and wince. Rancid and noxious and green, like no semen I've ever encountered, and I've encountered quite a lot of it, in my time. Worse, it's giving off a faint glow, casting a sickly viridian shadow on to the underside of our faces. I shudder and wipe the inside of my thighs with the sheet.

'What did you put inside me, you fucking freak?'

This seems to confuse him even further, so I come out with it.

'I've been raped.'

He stares at me, long and hard, before shaking his head.

'Don't look at me. You're not my type.'

'You think rapists only rape their *type*?'

'Who says it was rape?'

'I don't remember consenting.'

'Babe, I didn't touch you,' he says. 'I'm not that desperate.'

I can't believe he's smiling. I feel like smashing his face in.

'Don't call me babe.'

'OK. Girl. Woman. Whatever.'

He's a prick, that much is clear, but I force myself to simmer down because we're in the same boat, unless he really is playing a sadistic game. But I don't think so. His act is too convincing, and now even the obnoxiousness is leaking out of him, leaving him a punctured balloon of bewilderment.

'Maybe we did have sex,' he says. 'I don't remember.'

'What *do* you remember?'

We question each other, tentatively, like a couple on a first date. We each remember growing up, going to school. We remember our names. I remember being picture editor on a magazine. He remembers working as a trainee chef. But beyond that, our memories are fogged, as though someone opened the door to the darkroom of our minds before the images could be fixed. All I can summon are vague sensations, but I can't sort them into any sort of context. We don't *think* we've ever met before, but we can't be sure. Maybe we did meet, and that's just another of the things we've forgotten.

One thing I do know. 'I drank too much.'

He nods. 'Me too. I take it you *don't* have paracetamol.'

I tell him there might be some in my bag, but I don't know where it is. I can't see a bag here. But at least I've remembered something. I do have a bag. Or *had* one. So where is it now?

I try to lick my lips, but there's not enough moisture in my mouth to do it efficiently. I would sell my soul for a drink of water. My gaze wanders longingly across the room, towards the basin where the glass is waiting to be filled... But it's an impossible dream. I'm still not capable of standing up, let alone walking all the way over there.

And then, scattered fragments come back to me. Running down some backstairs, stumbling, laughing. A castle in ruins. Picking my way over rubble towards the gateway to a city. Something on fire. Maybe a car, or a person. Twisting, tearing, screaming...

I attempt to put these impressions into words, but they resist so stubbornly I give up. 'Probably a dream.'

'Wait,' he says. He screws up his face in concentration. 'The sound of breaking glass, right? Running down a long staircase? I remember that too. Dark streets, flashing lights...'

'Did we dream the same thing?' I begin to shiver so hard my teeth knock together. Up until now my terror has been blunted by befuddlement, but now it forces its way through the numbness and hits me, hard. The windowless room suddenly feels smaller, the walls closing in on us. I need to get out of here right now. Where are my clothes? They must be here somewhere. I lean over the edge of the bed, and my head swims as the pattern on the carpet comes up to meet me with its interlocking semi-abstract swirls which might be flowers, or birds with sharpened beaks. And I'm struck by the feeling – no, the *absolute conviction* – that I've done all this before. But that's not possible. How could I *not* remember a hangover this bad?

For a moment I feel so dizzy I think I'm going to have to lie flat again, but finally my eyes pick out something that isn't part of the pattern. I reach out and grasp the edge of a limp bundle of fabric, and pull it up on to the bed. A dress? But something's not right. I try to smooth it out. Was a dress. Now streaked with rust-coloured stains, and in tatters. As though shredded by claws.

'Jesus.' He pokes at the mangled fabric with his finger. 'What happened?'

'Hang on. There's more.' This time I almost tumble on to the floor trying to reach the rest of the clothes, but he holds on to my waist as I pull them up on to the bed. Or what's left of them. We sift listlessly through the pile, trying in vain to reassemble the stained scraps into viable memories. He finally locates what appears to be a pocket and slides his fingers into it hopefully, but the only thing in there is a blue cigarette lighter.

'Something attacked us,' I say.

There's an outbreak of growling, so loud I peer around fearfully, thinking whatever shredded our clothes must be right here with us, in the room. Only when he looks embarrassed do I realise the sound is coming from his abdomen.

'Sorry,' he says. 'I'm starving.'

'Me too,' I say. 'And thirsty. Spitting feathers.'

We both look longingly at the basin, so distant it might as well be on Mars. I grit my teeth, ignore the pain, and set my feet on the carpet, but before I can go any further I'm hit by another wave of debilitating nausea. Nausea, and something else I can't quite put my finger on. Something else I don't *want* to put my finger on, as though I'm in the grip of something bigger and more powerful, something which is watching and laughing, having fun at our expense.

I keel sideways, defeated. He sighs as though I've let us both down.

'At least I tried,' I say.

He interprets this as a reproach, and laboriously swings his legs over the side of the bed in his turn. I slide over to watch his slow progress. I really want him to stand, so he can fetch me some water, but already he's in trouble. His mouth contorts, and for a second I think he's going to throw up, but instead he sinks slowly to his knees and lowers his head till all I can see of him is his back. But I can hear him muttering, 'Close to the earth...'

His shoulders tense up. Even though I can't see his face from here, I can tell he's spotted something.

Then, in a muffled voice, 'We have a bag.'

A bag! I feel a flush of triumph. Surely the bag will provide answers. There'll be clues in it. Maybe even a phone.

He makes a strangled noise in his throat, and when he turns to look up at me, I wish he hadn't. All the blood has drained out of his face, leaving the skin looking like greaseproof paper.

'Something else... I can't... You'd better get down here.'

I'm still feeling optimistic about the bag, so even though I don't like the look on his face I slither off the bed until I'm kneeling alongside him. So long as I have my head down I can keep the nausea at bay. Now I understand what he meant by *close to the earth*. Close to the earth is where we need to be.

Down here, on the floor, the sweet and sour smell is stronger, and the humming's so loud it's making my eardrums vibrate. The effort of moving has sapped what little energy was available to me, and the yellow light barely penetrates the shadows, so it's another moment or two before my eyes can make out the object on the floor.

A leather tote bag, tan and weathered, another yellow Post-it stuck to the side. I unpeel the note and bring it up close to squint at the same spindly printing.

IF HUNGER'S MAKING YOU FEEL WEAK
UNDER THE BED IS WHAT YOU SEEK

My stomach gurgles in response. I *am* hungry. Maybe there's something to eat in the bag, an energy bar, something like that. I grab the worn leather strap and tug at it.

The bag is heavier than it looks, but it bumps across the carpet towards me. I prepare to unzip it and look inside.

The man touches my arm.

'Not that,' he whispers. '*That.*'

He's shaking his head and pointing at something beyond the bag, so I let go of the strap and peer into the shadows.

What *is* that? A side of beef, or pork? Raw and bloody. Frills of skin and trailing flaps, not a clean cut at all. Something smooth and white sticking out of the top. What the hell is a big chunk of meat doing here under the bed? It should be in the fridge. In any case it's uncooked, so we can't eat it.

Overcome by curiosity, I stretch out an arm, about to prod the joint when my gaze drifts to the other end and I snatch my hand back and, even though it never made contact, wipe it convulsively on the carpet.

The meat tapers off into a plimsoll. A man's plimsoll, judging by the size of it. A plimsoll and a sticky red sock. No, not red but grey. Grey drenched in red, like the carpet beneath it.

'At least now we know where the blood came from,' I say, trying not to giggle and wondering at the same time why on earth I would find this funny.

'Who put it here?' he asks, as if I'd know any better than him. I ask myself again if he's feigning ignorance, because there's something about this situation that feels off.

I shake this nonsense out of my head. Of *course* it feels off. In what world would a leg under the bed feel normal? Hoping the bag will provide answers, I prepare once again to unzip it, but he frowns and says, 'No, don't open that.'

But this just makes me all the more determined, so I grasp the sides of the leather and feel it throbbing softly, and only now do I realise the humming has been coming from inside the bag all along. Has to be a phone inside, making that sound! So I pull on the zip and look inside, and reality abruptly shifts into another, darker dimension.

He's watching me apprehensively, so I try to explain. 'I thought it was a phone.' Not sure how to put into words what I'm seeing, I push the bag over so he can look for himself. He peers inside, and his eyes widen, but he keeps staring, as though he can't rip his gaze away.

At last, he says, 'Why is it making that noise?'

'Maybe it's fake.' I'm clutching at straws here.

'Looks real enough to me.' He looks at the leg. 'Same person?'

Christ, let's hope so. One set of body parts is bad enough. He reaches into the bag and for a ghastly moment I think he's going to pull the severed head out by its hair, but instead he unpeels the yellow Post-it from the forehead and reads the words out loud.

THE GAME'S AFOOT! THE HEAD'S IN PLAY
A LIGHTED FLAME WILL SHOW THE WAY

We stare at each other, searching for some sort of explanation, but all we see are mirror images of our own disbelief.

The yellow light flickers. Once, twice.

Our heads swivel towards the light fitting. It flickers again, more rapidly now. Each time it blinks, the light grows dimmer, the shadows longer.

'Oh crap,' I say, because the idea of being trapped in darkness with that *thing*, these *things*, this man I don't know from Adam and who may yet be a psychopath, fills me with a dread more primal than any I've been feeling up till now.

He's still holding the Post-it Note.

A LIGHTED FLAME

'There's a candle over there,' I say.

'Worth a try,' he says, and in the rapidly dwindling light I sense rather than see him get to his feet with suspicious ease. Not such an invalid now, eh. Maybe he thought I wouldn't notice, but now he dives towards the chest of drawers and grabs the putty-coloured candle in its holder.

'Lighter!' he barks.

For a second I mistake his meaning and think he's issuing a godlike command. Then I understand, and grope around on the bed until my fingers close around the blue cigarette lighter, which I scoop up and fling in the direction of his voice, thinking there is *no way* he'll see that small object flying through the dying light towards him, and how did I manage to throw it so accurately anyway? But in an impossibly quick movement, he plucks it out of the air, as though some long-forgotten instinct as a cricket fielder has welled up inside him and repossessed his hand. In a smooth, practised movement, he flicks the lighter and holds the flame to the wick of the candle, which flares up and casts an eerie flickering around the room.

The light is no longer yellow but the colour of dry oatmeal infested with weevils. Something else in the room has changed. There's another presence here.

He turns back to me, looking smug. 'We make a good team.'

'Well, that was odd,' I say, as though everything up until now has been normal. I don't know where we found that energy, but the sudden burst of activity has left us more enervated than ever. He flops back down, so now we're both kneeling naked in front of the bag, like supplicants at an oracle.

The humming gets louder and the flickering light turns

from oatmeal to greenish, but it's not just the candle lighting the room now. The head in the bag is glowing. I try to put a name to the colour emanating from it, but all I can come up with is *bile*.

The dead eyes flick open. The dead lips vibrate, and the humming forms itself into words.

'Ask me while I'm still aglow. I'll tell you all you need to know.'

The man and I look at each other. It's the closest I've felt to him yet and, in a way, I'm relieved he's there because I'm not sure I could cope with this on my own. And yet, there's a buried part of me which is finding this new development hilarious. I suspect that part is insanity, and know instinctively that I mustn't laugh, or I'll unleash it into the room. Not that there isn't enough insanity here to begin with.

The head is staring at us, but blankly. It isn't seeing anything. Or rather, it *is* seeing something – something that might have once been here, but isn't any longer.

The man next to me clears his throat and addresses it, as though talking to a severed head is the most natural thing in the world.

'Who did this?'

The lips move. In its humming, vibrating mockery of a voice, it says, 'You want to know who made this mess? Your hands are red, so take a guess.'

'No!' says my companion.

'Your memory is just a blur. You don't remember what you were.'

'My name is Elizabeth,' I tell it. 'I'm a picture editor.'

The lips peel back until I see blood on the teeth.

'Once upon a distant past, in bodies never built to last.'

My male companion persists. 'We've never met before.'

The head rolls its eyes, revealing not whites but yellow jelly.

'Your bond is forged in pain and blood, in fire and water, air and mud.'

'Why should we listen to you?' I have to stifle that hysterical laughter again.

'You knew you'd wander off the track and tasked me to direct you back.'

I've had enough of this. I say to my companion, 'I vote we close the bag and kick it back under the bed,' hoping he'll take the hint and zip up the bag for the both of us, because I have no intention of touching that throbbing leather sac again, not now, not ever.

'I'm inclined to agree with you,' he says. 'We don't need this... this *thing* ordering us around.'

The head rolls its eyes again. 'Remembering can set you free, but hey, it's all the same to me.'

The man says, 'What if we don't *want* to remember?'

The head makes a chuckling noise, and hacks up a small quantity of green fluid which reminds me of the stuff I found between my legs. I find myself wondering how it can cough when its respiratory tract has been shorn off at the neck, and feel sick all over again.

'If you refuse to seek the thread, you'll end up wishing you were dead.'

'OK then,' I say. 'Tell us what we need to know.' I'm just humouring it now, because I have no intention of letting this *abomination* boss us around.

'To clear your mind and stop the pain...' Its voice seems to be fading. 'Drink, digest, get dressed again...'

I blurt out, 'Our clothes are all torn and covered in blood!'

'The *clean* clothes folded in the drawer...'

'How do you know what's in there?'

It sighs. 'You laid out everything beforrrrr...'

It gets stuck on the syllable, like a gramophone needle stuck in the same groove, coughs up blood again and the vibrations we mistook for a voice die away along with the last of the humming. The eyes close. And the bile-coloured glow fades, leaving the face waxy and dead, the only movement now from the flickering beige candlelight playing across its pallid contours.

Without the humming the room seems unnaturally peaceful. I feel like clambering on to the bed and going back to sleep. This is all a dream, and when I wake up it'll all be back to normal... Whatever normal is, and I'm not sure any more. But I'm too thirsty. What was it the head said? Drink? Digest?

I look at my companion and he looks back at me. Is it my imagination or does his face seem more familiar now? Have we really met before? Or maybe we only know each other from the past ten minutes, which seem to have stretched into a lifetime of pain, and hunger, and thirst.

'Water,' he says.

I'm filled with foreboding. 'No, wait.'

He ignores me, lifts himself on to his hands and knees, and begins to crawl on all fours towards the basin. No, not crawl; more like *scuttling*, like a misshapen insect. He's moving unnaturally fast, genitalia swinging from side to side, or maybe it just seems fast to me because I'm still rooted to the spot. The trust I was beginning to place in him has withered. So I follow him, reluctantly. I sense this is a trap, and I'm crawling straight into it, but there's no going back now.

He reaches the basin and, grunting with the effort, hauls

himself up. By the time I join him there, his fingers are already closing around the glass tumbler, as though it was the prize in a contest I've just lost. 'No, wait,' I say again, but he picks it up and twists the tap. There's a whine of protest from the ancient plumbing, and water trickles into the glass, with a sound like music.

He waits until it's filled to the brim before saying, 'Here we go,' turning towards me with a half-apologetic smile and tipping back his head and pouring the contents of the glass into his mouth, Adam's apple bobbing as he swallows, water running down his chin, dripping on to his chest.

I paw at his arm, but he shrugs me off, drains the tumbler and lowers his head, looking straight at me with a malicious gleam in his eyes as his fingers tighten, knuckles turning white, fist gripping tighter and tighter until there's a loud crack and the glass disintegrates into a million splinters.

'You bastard,' I say.

He lets the splinters fall, picks slivers out of his palm and drops the biggest shards into the basin. Then holds up his bleeding hand, spreading the fingers so I can see the blood trickling down his arm.

'Looks like I won,' he says.

If I weren't so dehydrated I'd be weeping with fury. I lean over the basin and poke at the remains of the glass, but not a single piece is big enough to hold even a tiny amount of the water now trickling uselessly down the plughole.

Before I can think about what to do next, there's an animal screech behind me. I look in the mirror. Beyond the reflection of my face, shiny and alien, I can see him still clutching his bleeding hand. But the image is rippling. His skin is erupting into goose pimples so big they cast shadows like hills on an illustrated map. His fingernails are growing.

His face contorts with agony as his eyes sink further and further into his skull until the sockets are dark pools. I sway dangerously, shaking my head, but the image is still there. At last the rippling stops and his mouth spreads into an impossibly wide smile, showing more teeth than a mouth has any right to hold.

'What the hell,' I say, and make the mistake of turning round to face him, assuming the reflection in the mirror is distorted and that when I see him for real he'll look normal again.

Except he doesn't.

'Come to daddy,' he says, beckoning with fingernails now like vicious twigs. His voice has changed. Now it sounds as though it's coming from a deep dark place beneath our feet. His toenails are growing too, each one curved, like a Turkish scimitar.

'Fuck no.' I retreat as far as I can into the corner by the basin, wishing I could disappear. I'm beginning to understand. The other guy, the one I woke up with, didn't attack me. But this one did. And this one isn't a man at all. I don't know what he is.

When he laughs, the sound is like nails rattling in a can.

I brace myself for another onslaught, but instead of attacking me again he tips his head to one side, as if responding to a distant call my ears can't hear, and turns to move away from me, towards the bed, where he sinks to his knees in a supple movement, not at all like his earlier collapse. He reaches under the bed and draws out the leg, clamps his teeth into the fatty part of the calf, and begins to chew.

My empty stomach heaves at the sight, but at least the meat has bought me time. I stumble to the door and turn the handle. Locked. In frustration I bang my forehead against the wood, dislodging the yellow Post-it clinging there. It floats to the floor before I get a chance to read the words on it.

There's an explosion of moist laughter at my ear. He's left the bed and is standing right behind me. It's the laugh of someone with his mouth full, spitting shreds of meat and saliva. At the same instant I feel a scything pain across my shoulder, as though I've caught it in a sliding door, followed by a tightness in my lungs and a shock of freezing air, and wetness spilling out. I fall to my knees, as if someone has snipped the thread that has been holding me upright.

But at least now I'm down here I can read the Post-it.

THE END IS NEARER THAN YOU THINK
THE ONLY THING TO DO IS DRINK

Yes, that's all very well, and I'm literally dying of thirst, but there's no fucking glass. Not any more.

Hysterical laughter wells up inside me once again. Who cares if there isn't a glass, stupid? I can still hear water trickling out of the tap. I begin to crawl back towards the ever more distant basin, and everything is getting darker, and I'm aware it isn't the light that's fading this time; it's my eyesight. Glass splinters embed themselves into my hands and knees, but I try to ignore the stinging pain, and keep moving, head down like a purposeful household pet moving towards its feeding bowl. Can I reach the basin before I bleed to death and the light goes out for ever?

'I know you're there!' he says.

Of course I'm there. Where else would I be, for fuck's sake? But he's moved again, and without me even noticing. Now he's towering over me. He raises his arm, sending a long dark shadow racing across the ceiling, and I can feel the air being displaced with a whoosh as the fingernails swoop down. I manage to twist sideways so they miss my neck, but instead they sink into the soft flesh of my abdomen. He doesn't draw them out, but screws them deeper, exploring, until I can feel them grasping something and pulling it out. I look down and see grey coils spilling out of a deep, dark hole hemmed by wayward flaps of shredded skin. As I watch in horrified fascination, the hole wells up with viscous brown liquid which overflows and drips out and is absorbed into the carpet. This is me, or what's left of me, and soon there will be nothing left.

I resume my epic crawl towards the basin, because the alternative is to curl up and bleed, or be eaten alive or dismembered. Who knows, maybe he'll decapitate me and put my head in a bag. Maybe I'll end up glowing bile-green and speaking words I don't understand to other people who don't understand them.

I must have blacked out but suddenly I'm there, the washbasin looming over me like a grimy porcelain stump. I wrap my failing arms around the pedestal and pull myself up, slithering in my own blood in a big fat parody of a pole dance. And then I'm slumped over the basin, watching my blood circling the plughole. Thank god he didn't shut the tap off, because I don't think I would have had enough strength left to turn it on.

The dripping blood forms fuzzy-edged tributaries which branch out and rejoin each other in a delta of gore. The sight is so mesmerising I almost forget why I'm there. But then it comes back to me. Ah yes. *The only thing to do is drink.*

More laughter, this time from right behind my ear. I can smell his rank and meaty breath as his teeth snap like scissors close to my neck. Just as his fingers seize my left arm and start to pull it out of its socket, I manage to dip my head beneath the tap so water trickles into my open mouth. At first there seems too much of it, and it makes me cough and splutter. But then some of the wetness leaks into my parched throat, soaking into the cracks until my insides are filling out and swelling up, all pink and plump and juicy again. Then I swallow.

The effect is instantaneous. I feel more like my old self again. The putty-coloured candle flares up one last time and goes out. But it doesn't matter. Light or dark, it's all the same to us now.

And now I know everything. I know it will take another few hours for the wounds to heal, but heal they will, and I can already feel my torn flesh knitting itself back together, like a million pins and needles in a sewing factory. One by one, the ruptured veins and arteries are sealing themselves. It's a good feeling, the strength seeping back, and then even more strength. Inhuman strength. I look down fondly at the grey loops extruding from my torso, feeling an urge to play cat's cradle with them before they heal. So badly fashioned, these bodies. All those fragile tubes and layers, flapping uselessly around.

And there's more. I can feel my fingernails growing longer and sharper, like his. I straighten up and stretch like a big cat and turn to greet him with a wide smile, showing off my rows of new teeth.

'I was beginning to think you'd never make it,' he says in his new voice.

'Christ, I'm starving.' My voice sounds like his, deep and dark and guttural. Not my voice at all. Correction, it *is* mine. This is my *real* voice. The other one was just a placeholder.

Together, we finish off the leg, which has a gamey taste, but it doesn't matter because it's still delicious, and when we've eaten that, we start on the head. We reach into the bag and prise off the top of the skull with our fingernails and pull out chunks and stuff them into our mouths. It's like a panettone full of juicy sultanas and crunchy bits of cranium.

When the bag is empty, our stomachs are still roiling with hunger, but our body clocks inform us it's after midnight. Feeding time. The leg and head were just an amuse-bouche. Time to go out on the town again, drinking and dancing and crashing cars, setting things on fire and eating people. The usual stuff.

Before we go, we kiss, long and deep. His tongue snakes all the way down my throat and tickles my lungs. Mine worms its way up through the back of his nose into his brain and lingers there, lapping at the lobes from the inside, and I look forward to tasting his greasy green semen again, and laugh with delight, remembering how earlier I found it so repulsive. What a fool I was. It's not repulsive at all. It's a delicacy.

For a while, we feel our way around each other's bodies. Our *real* bodies, not the stupid ones we were lumbered with. They'll be back, probably. I certainly hope so. Maybe we'll regress every now and again and be obliged to grope around blindly, desperately seeking our true selves, but we'll carry on leaving Post-its and severed body parts to point the way back. And I know the clues will never stop being cryptic, because tormenting those other selves is all part of the fun. So feeble. So useless. So *stupid*. How could you *not* want to torture them?

We lick the last of the blood off each other. Then open the drawers and find the clothes where we left them several aeons ago, clean and neatly folded. They're rough and grey, like army surplus. We put them on, and then the greatcoats, which smell of nutmeg, and inspect each other with mutual admiration.

'Good to have you back,' he says.

'Good to *be* back,' I say.

On the way to the door, I pause to examine the dark picture on the wall. Up close, I can finally make out an intricate tangle of human figures, some with bird or animal heads, others sinking into black pits or trussed to spiked wheels. Nails hammered into tendons, entrails spilling out in steaming coils, heads roasting like chestnuts, mouths gaping in inaudible screams, and... something else.

'Hey!' I say, pointing at two smiling figures holding saws, poised in the act of removing one victim's legs from the rest of his torso. 'They look just like us!'

He grins. 'So they do. Shall we go?'

I could stare at that amusement park of pain all night, but he wrenches the locked door open with a flick of the wrist, leaving the jamb in splinters, and extends his arm towards me in invitation. I take it as we step outside.

It feels good to be us.

CONTRIBUTORS & ACKNOWLEDGEMENTS

Jenn Ashworth is an award-winning novelist and short story writer. Her latest novel, *Fell*, is published by Sceptre.

Anne Billson is a writer, photographer and film critic. Her books include four horror novels: *Suckers*, *Stiff Lips*, *The Ex* and *The Coming Thing*.

David Gaffney is the author of several books, including *Sawn-off Tales*, *Aromabingo*, *Never Never*, *The Half-life of Songs*, *More Sawn-off Tales*, *All The Places I've Ever Lived* and graphic novel *The Three Rooms in Valerie's Head*.

Jessie Greengrass studied philosophy in Cambridge and London. Her short story collection, *An Account of the Decline of the Great Auk, According to One Who Saw It*, won the 2016 Edge Hill Short Story Prize and a Somerset Maugham Award. Her novel, *Sight*, was shortlisted for the 2018 Women's Prize for Fiction.

Zoe Lambert lectures in creative writing at Lancaster University. Her debut collection of stories, *The War Tour*, was published by Comma Press in 2012.

Toby Litt is the author of ten novels, including *deadkidsongs*, *Ghost Story* and *Notes for a Young Gentleman*, and four short story collections. His most recent book is *Wrestliana*. He lectures in creative writing at Birkbeck, University of London.

Sophie Mackintosh was the winner of the 2016 White Review Short Story Prize and the 2016 Stylist Virago Short Story Prize, and was shortlisted for the 2017 Berlin Writing Prize. Her fiction has appeared in *Granta* and *TANK*. Her debut novel, *The Water Cure*, is published by Hamish Hamilton.

Zoë McLean is a graphic designer, film-maker, typesetter and illustrator based in Manchester.

Louise Marr is a graduate of the Creative Writing MA at the University of Manchester. Her stories have been short-listed for the Asham Award and the Mslexia Women's Short Story Award. 'Interzone' is her first published story.

Nicholas Royle is the author of three short story collections – *Mortality* (shortlisted for the 2007 Edge Hill Short Story Prize), *Ornithology* (longlisted for the 2018 Edge Hill Prize) and *The Dummy & Other Uncanny Stories* – and seven novels. He is series editor of *Best British Short Stories*. Reader in Creative Writing at the Manchester Writing School and head judge of the Manchester Fiction Prize, he also runs Nightjar Press.

Eley Williams is currently Writer in Residence at the University of Greenwich. Her debut collection, *Attrib. and other stories*, was listed among best books of 2017 by the *Guardian*, the *Telegraph* and the *New Statesman*, and chosen by Ali Smith as one of the year's best debut works of fiction at the Cambridge Literary Festival. It was also awarded the 2018 Republic of Consciousness Prize, has been shortlisted for the 2018 James Tait Black Memorial Prize and was longlisted for the 2018 Edge Hill Short Story Prize.

ACKNOWLEDGEMENTS

I would like to thank the following people for their help in producing this book: Jenn Ashworth, Karen Clarke, David Gaffney, Hannah Hargrave, Karl Hildebrandt, Hoss, Zoë McLean, Ben Myers, Scott Pack, Janet Penny, Nicholas Royle, Anokhi Shah, Tim Shearer, Lisa Snook and Katie Taylor.

All of the stories that make up *We Were Strangers*, together with the graphic interlude, were written specially for this anthology and are published here for the first time. While no quotation from the lyrics of *Unknown Pleasures* is used in the stories, the music publisher, Universal Music Publishing Group, has been notified of the publication of the book.

The quotations from Ian Rankin and Irvine Welsh first appeared in *The Quietus*.

RICHARD V. HIRST

ORIGINAL ILLUSTRATION, DESIGN & TYPESETTING
Zoë McLean, Manchester
zoe@confingopublishing.uk

FONTS
Baskerville, Futura

PAPER
90gsm Munken Premium Cream

PRINTING & BINDING
TJ International, Cornwall
tjinternational.ltd.uk